A Touch of Silence & Other Tales

Simon Bleaken

Copyright © 2017 Simon Bleaken

Cover Image: Adobe Stock UK
© andreiuc88 ID #69944458

All rights reserved.
ISBN: 1542594561
ISBN-13: 978-1542594561

Dedication

This book is dedicated to three people without whom many of these stories might never have been.

Jonathan Self,
Hilary Deighton
and David Lee Summers

"Sigil of Komashin" first appeared in *Tales of the Talisman Vol 5 Issue 4*, edited by David Lee Summers, copyright © 2010 by Simon Bleaken.

"Touch of Silence" first appeared in *Tales of the Talisman Vol 8 Issue 1*, edited by David Lee Summers, copyright © 2012 by Simon Bleaken.

"The Fourth Setting" first appeared in *Tales of the Talisman Vol 10 Issue 3*, edited by David Lee Summers, copyright © 2015 by Simon Bleaken.

"Regressives" first appeared in *Tales of the Talisman Vol 9 Issue 1*, edited by David Lee Summers, copyright © 2013 by Simon Bleaken.

"Automated Relay" first appeared in *Tales of the Talisman Vol 10 Issue 1*, edited by David Lee Summers, copyright © 2014 by Simon Bleaken.

"Draystone's Secret" first appeared in *Tales of the Talisman Vol 10 Issue 4*, edited by David Lee Summers, copyright © 2015 by Simon Bleaken.

"Thornway Hollow" first appeared in *Tales of the Talisman Vol 9 Issue 3*, edited by David Lee Summers, copyright © 2014 by Simon Bleaken.

"The Tree By The Well" copyright © 2015 by Simon Bleaken.

"Natural Selection" first appeared in *Space Horrors: Full Throttle Space Tales #4*, edited by David Lee Summers, copyright © 2010 by Simon Bleaken.

"Sidhe Brook" first appeared in *Tales of the Talisman Vol 7 Issue 3*, edited by David Lee Summers, copyright © 2012 by Simon Bleaken.

Contents

The Sigil of Komashin	9
Touch of Silence	28
The Fourth Setting	45
Regressives	65
Automated Relay	86
Draystone's Secret	107
Thornway Hollow	126
The Tree By The Well	146
Natural Selection	167
Sidhe Brook	188

The Sigil of Komashin

The meridian sun cast feeble, heatless rays upon the darkly huddled buildings of the ancient city of Wevven, and into the winding and narrow avenues that coiled serpent-like between them. The light that sparkled on the heavy, igneous rocks of the tall buildings, glinting on the minerals trapped within, were the dying rays of a sun on the verge of burning out. On the outskirts of the oval city, great dolmens and obelisks erected in ages past reared skyward with a bleak majesty; relics of an age when the sun shone brightly, the land was green and fertile, and the rivers ran cool and deep with fast-flowing waters teeming with fish. Now, the failing sun had cast a shadow of chill death upon the land. The plants were dying, and the animals were growing ever scarcer – mere scavengers, picking a desperate survival from the scant food sources that remained.

The barren land outside the city was seldom visited anymore. The great tombs and monuments of ages past lay forgotten and crumbling – though at night the darkness was alive with moving shadows. For in the black recesses outside the walls and barred gates, prowling and lurking for any unwise enough to venture beyond the city's protection and ever seeking a way inside, the vampires waited: gaunt, lean and inhumanly pale, with piercing eyes like blazing yellow opals and blood-red lips concealing sharp fangs. Like all the inhabitants of this doomed world, they were slowly starving, and whilst the failing sunlight was a boon to them, the gradual extinction and thinning of the remaining life denied them the blood they craved so desperately. Now, they screamed and howled, clawing at the walls with their long nails and fighting amongst themselves like feral beasts over any living creature that foolishly wandered into their midst.

It was a once-great civilisation that had passed beyond the zenith of its development and had begun the long and gradual slide into decadence, decay and eventual dissolution; the golden ages of the past now but an ancient memory preserved by crumbling tomes and frail umber parchments. And with the passing of the sun, the gravity that held the planet in check would be gone – and cold darkness would claim the world as it drifted away through the limitless void of space as a mere lifeless rock, its rich history and people a lost memory.

But in Wevven, for now, life still struggled against the inevitable. In the heart of the crowded city, where lofty towers of dark angular basalt topped with verdigris-covered bronze spires rose sharply into the hazy air, lay the central ziggurat of the sun god Agralis, dominating all that lay around it. Here, on a daily basis, the solemn grey-robed priests, their faces hidden beneath heavy hoods and a vow of silence upon their lips, lit braziers and poured libations of wine and water in the anxious hope that Agralis would not abandon them and would ease their suffering. In their hearts the priests understood the science that lay behind the failing of the sun – but they also knew that with the proper incantations and rituals, Agralis himself could be placated into taking action, restoring the balance that would make the sun thrive again. In the past the fourteen gods of Berradis had been worshipped equally in their own shrines atop this mighty monument – revered for their gifts of science and sorcery that they had bestowed upon the mortals of the lands below. But with the failing of the sun, and the inability of either science or magic to solve the crisis, worship of Agralis had increased exponentially, to the near exclusion of the other gods – a state that had greatly concerned many theologians, who feared that the wrathful jealousy of the other deities might bring further dire catastrophe upon the already beleaguered civilisation. Stories abounded from the elder days of the terrible curses to befall those who mocked or showed disrespect to the gods: babies born with ophidian heads, people struck with madness or blindness, or stricken with ailments that crippled or disfigured the body. It was even believed – though still disputed by some – that the vampires had been born of such a curse.

Such concerns were foremost in the mind of one individual now hurrying through the tightly winding streets. Jaraxl Debier pushed his way through the gathered multitudes that milled in solemn and sombre silence around the great agora, casting wary glances around for any sign that the city guards had spotted him. Of course, it was impossible that they could know of his plan, or have any reason to suspect that he was about to commit an act that was tantamount to treason in the eyes of the Ruling Assembly – but still his heart was racing at the prospect of what lay ahead, and his throat had gone horribly dry.

Jaraxl caught a guard's eye as he hurried out into Wevven's agora, and glanced quickly away – a little too quickly. As he moved through the joyless crowd, trying to slip inconspicuously amongst their number, he thought he saw the guard tense and strain to get a better look – and immediately wanted to kick himself for his stupidity.

Easy - calm and slow, he thought, the words becoming almost a mantra as he eased himself behind one of the market stalls. A second glance back and he allowed himself to relax - the guard had resumed his post up on the ramparts, and was impassively scanning the thronging crowd once more. Keeping a watchful eye out for any other guards, Jaraxl wound his way through market stalls once redolent with exotic spices and tobacco, or resplendent with silks, figs, tiger nuts and dates, but which now had a forlorn and threadbare look to them. The harvests and produce of recent years had not been kind, and a desolation born of melancholy, fear and brooding uncertainty hung thickly over the solemn agora. Even the great theatre, hewn from the bedrock itself, was silent and had gone unused for decades.

He caught a glimpse of a face in the crowd then – Salla – one of his colleagues.

"It's done," she whispered, surreptitiously passing him a small object wrapped in rough linen, before slipping back into the sea of bodies and disappearing from view.

It was time to make his move. The guards had been pulled away from the doors, but they wouldn't leave their posts for long.

He swallowed hard as he tucked the object into his robe, fighting back a nervous wave of fear, and then hurried toward the imposing and dismal bulk of the Ruling Assembly's labyrinthine complex – a sprawling warren of immense structures just beyond the agora that housed both the government chambers, and the restricted divisions of scientific and arcane research. To be caught inside any of the restricted areas without proper authority or a permit was a crime that carried the immediate penalty of death.

It was a risk Jaraxl had to take. Everything depended upon it.

As he neared the colossal black doors to the complex he noted that Salla and her friends had done their job well – the guards were nowhere to be seen, and the arcane wards engraved into the ebony wood had been temporarily neutralized. It took only a few seconds for him to haul one of the doors open and slip quickly inside, but as it closed behind him he knew that in those few fleeting moments a line had been crossed - and from this point on, if he failed, his life was forfeit.

With a heart heavy with fearful responsibility and anxious dread, he crept through the barren, echoing passageways, keeping a watchful eye for any internal guard patrols, his thick cloak pulled tightly around his tattered burnoose to fend off the growing chill of the morning. It was always cold here now, and the winters had grown progressively harsh and bitter. The mild summers of Jaraxl's childhood were now a thing of distant memory.

He glanced quickly around at a sudden sound from behind him, a surge of alarm rising as he peered into the shadowy recesses of the hallway, before forcing himself to relax. If the city guard had discovered his illegal access into the sealed catacombs, they would be swarming through them by now – and he would have received warning from both Salla and her associates keeping a hidden watch at the entrance.

He turned a corner, descended down a long gloomy staircase of heavy stone, and through a set of doors at the bottom. He knew he was entering the oldest part of the complex – constructed thousands of years earlier, when the schools of science and sorcery were in their infancy. The dark and heavy hallways ran out from where he stood with an uncannily machine-straight precision, tracing the cardinal points and terminating in dark, steeply corbelled chambers burdened by the weight of their aeons-old construction and the countless tons of stone that they held aloft. Far below, in the dank, shadowy crypts and domed vaults, festooned with dust and cobwebs, the silence of ages lay heavy upon the crumbling mummified remains of the ancient, interred dead: the chief scientists and mages of past generations, lying in state in their cerements of mouldering silks and rich velvet, bedecked with heavy golden amulets and dusty gemstones.

Jaraxl had now penetrated the heart of the catacombs, and knew his destination lay close at hand – but even he was unprepared for the sight of the great bronze doors, or the effect they would have upon him as he beheld them. They rose up to the ceiling, towering twice his height and tapering inward at the top. Each was intricately inlaid with lapis lazuli, feldspar, amethyst, carnelian and turquoise all arranged in a delicate and cryptically esoteric pattern over the surface. Trying to calm his apprehensive, quickening heart, he scurried over to them and pressed his hand against the cool metal. He had hardly dared to believe that he would make it this far. He had been certain that something would have gone wrong, or been overlooked, leading to his swift capture and execution. But he *had* made it, and now stood at the very doors to Komashin's legendary chamber, and quite possibly, the salvation they all so desperately sought.

He turned the handle and stepped inside without a backward glance.

It was dark inside the cold chamber, and it took a while for his eyes to adjust enough to the gloom for him to find his way over to one of several nearby benches, where he lit the ancient lamps one by one and cast illumination on a chamber that had not seen light in millennia. He also drew open the great shutters on the high-up windows and allowed thin shafts of pale daylight to filter in. Around him bookcases rose up to the high ceiling, crowded with rolls of disintegrating vellum parchments and musty tomes, whilst sagging shelves held aloft a curious burden of glass spheres, copper blocks etched with bizarre runes, and strange devices inset with glass and crystal - all draped with the dust and cobwebs of undisturbed centuries.

He quickly ascertained that the chamber in which he stood was a mere antechamber to Komashin's main laboratory – part library and part storage archive of the many discoveries that Komashin had made during his long lifetime. But Jaraxl knew that those discoveries would have to wait for a later time – right now, only one device mattered – and with his heart in his throat, he lifted one of the lamps and moved toward the set of doors into the main laboratory.

Komashin's main chamber was no less impressive than the antechamber had been - a large square room whose high roof angled sharply inwards overhead, resembling a hollow pyramid. The stone walls were covered in small patches of copper, like tiny covers, and in the centre of the room, atop a stone pedestal reached by six steps, lay the remarkable device that Jaraxl had come in search of. It was the colour of lustreless bronze, resembling an elliptical orb supported on a tripod whose sturdy legs were covered in a bizarre series of glass and crystal tubes and curious coils of silvery metal. Where the legs met the floor however, they branched out into a mass of copper conduits that snaked out across the flagstones of the chamber like fine roots on a plant, before disappearing into the walls.

In truth, nobody was exactly certain what this device was, or just what it would do. It was a forbidden and ancient relic that had been sealed away for so long that it had entered the misty realms of legend. Scholars had long speculated on the nature of the device, though few had ever seen it with their own eyes. Some feared it would destroy the planet, while others believed it would save it – harnessing mystic and physical energies to restore life to the sun. A minority even refused to accept that it existed, believing it to be nothing more than a myth – arguing that if something so old and powerful existed, the Ruling Assembly would not simply have locked it away.

Jaraxl and his associates, however, had come to understand differently, and knew all too well the reasons behind the short-sighted actions of the Ruling Assembly and the outdated laws they clung so fastidiously to. And whilst the advances of civilisation had bestowed many wondrous gifts — the tripling of the human lifespan, the discovery of the structure of living cells, the power to transmogrify base metals into gold, and cures for many of the most virulent diseases known — they had nothing that could benefit them in finding a solution for the current dilemma; nothing that could restore the power of the life-giving sun. It was an outrage that the Ruling Assembly had forbidden the activation of the one machine that might be able to save them all, simply because of the nature of its creator.

Komashin had been a legend of his time — revered and respected, though greatly feared, and it had taken the rest of the civilized world centuries to even begin to understand much of his work and research. But little of it had ever been utilized, for despite his brilliance, Komashin had been a vampire — and when this long-held secret had finally been discovered, he had been instantly stripped of his rank as senior advisor to the king, and promptly burned alive in the castle courtyard; his work considered a heresy against the gods. Now two thousand years had passed, and his machine had waited locked in a secured vault — kept safely isolated from the smooth sigil that would activate it. Of all of Komashin's many complex and marvellous inventions, this had been the only one to defy analysis — and it alone remained an enigma, save for a simple note from Komashin claiming that it somehow contained the means to save the planet from its eventual and inevitable oblivion. But fear and mistrust of vampires was deeply ingrained, and the Ruling Assembly, although permitting scholars to examine Komashin's myriad devices, had a strict policy that none of the technology could be actively used in the way that Komashin had created it.

Given the seriousness of the threat facing their world, however, Jaraxl had spent months pleading with the council once he had learned that the device was more than a legend. But he had seen his requests ignored by those in charge – people supposedly chosen to maintain law and order throughout the land, and ensure the best interests and safety of the populace; but in reality, the members of the Assembly cared only for elevating and maintaining their positions, even in these dark times - the politics of power storming blindly ahead, even to the detriment of all. Jaraxl had no time for such petty pretensions. What good was power and personal advancement in a dying world? These so-called 'leaders' - burdened by a driving pathological need to advance themselves at any cost, even stepping upon those around them and sacrificing friendships and loyalties in the single-minded scramble to get ahead - refused to listen to other opinions that were either not their own, or that did not match their hidden personal agendas.

The corruption of the ruling government was well known and deeply entrenched over millennia, and many had come to believe it was holding back efforts to seek a solution to the problems that loomed over the planet. So Jaraxl and four of his colleagues from the Science Directorate had taken matters into their own hands, risking imprisonment and execution – they had sought out the fabled machine that the vampire had created, in an effort to save their dying world.

Jaraxl now ascended the steps to the device itself, withdrawing from his robes the small object that Salla had handed to him in the agora – and unwrapping it to reveal a smooth black sigil of some unknown metal. Salla had managed to acquire it from deep within the locked archives on the far side of the complex. At the top of the device was a recess, offset to the right, that was the exact size and shape of the sigil he now held, and taking a trembling breath, he inserted it into the space.

With a shrill grinding, the topmost surface of the bronze globe split and parted outwards like the elytra of a beetle, revealing two deep grooves beneath, just large enough for human hands to slot into. At the same time a faint and barely perceptible rumbling came from somewhere in the heart of the machine, and a pale reddish light spilled upwards from the deep grooves. Jaraxl took a startled step backwards at this. Trained in the sciences, the magical elements of the device were unfamiliar and alien to him – but the notes they had illicitly acquired suggested that the general operation of the machine should be relatively simple, and were purely mechanical in nature. The actual processes that took place within were less clear, and stubbornly thwarted all attempts at analysis – either magical or scientific, and Jaraxl had no choice but to place his faith in the hands of Komashin's work. With his heart pounding and sweat breaking out across his brow, he fought the urge to turn and flee – and slipped his hands down into the grooves.

There was no pain. There was no real sensation at all, only vague warmth, like dipping his hands into a warm pool of water. But with his hands in place the machine appeared to increase power – the rumbling grew louder and the device itself started to vibrate. Overhead, long thin rods of burnished metal were descending from behind some of the copper covers set into the ceiling, and these began to turn with increasing speed, grinding and shaking.

Far below, Jaraxl watched the chamber coming to life around him with a mixture of mesmerized wonder and uneasy dread. Not only was he the first living being in centuries to see this machine, he was now witnessing events that nobody had *ever* seen – not even Komashin himself had lived to see his device activated.

In his mind, Jaraxl found himself connecting with the device – becoming aware of the power unlocking before him, and in an impossible way, using his own thoughts to guide and regulate the distribution of that power. He wasn't sure how he was doing it, but it was as if the machine were guiding and using him as an external component of its functioning.

The spinning metal shafts overhead were now crackling and snarling as static electricity arced between them, and shafts of purple light were lancing down from crystals that had extended from the ceiling.

The solid door to the chamber rumbled shut with a heavy clang – and an anxious flutter of apprehensive doubt played in Jaraxl's heart, but he forced himself to maintain his position. After all they'd gone through to get this far, he wasn't going to back out now.

The metal rods overhead span faster, and a strange black fluid bubbled through the glass tubes on the legs of the tripod before him. The diabolical rumbling from the heart of the machine grew stronger, causing dust and grit to sift down from the ceiling overhead.

Minutes passed like this – perhaps even hours. Gradually, a wearying fatigue crept insidiously upon Jaraxl. Soon, his whole body ached and his eyes were heavy with the call of sleep. He forced himself to stay awake, battling against the increasing urge to rest his eyes. His body was heavy and clumsy, and a headache burned fiercely within his skull. His arms, still engaged with the machine, were like lumps of lead attached to his shoulders, and his breath came in wheezing gasps.

Inside this chamber he lost all knowledge of the passage of time. It all merged into a single interminable stretch of monotonous waiting. In fact the only sign of the passing hours came from the faint sunlight filtering in through the grills far above, but eventually the already pale light dimmed, and the orange-red tinge of dusk appeared.

How long will this take? He wondered dimly, his arms and shoulders aching. The fatigue had grown overwhelming now. Clearly, he reasoned, the machine must be drawing energy from him in some fashion. Even through the weariness that was upon him, a concern blossomed. How much of his strength would the machine need to complete its task? And how long would he need to remain attached to it? Komashin's notes had not specified any of those details, and in their haste to gain access to the device, they had not thought about it. Peering closely at the globe before him, he now dimly registered a small row of ruby-coloured lights that had commenced illuminating, one by one, along the bottom of the device. They were lighting up in succession as the machine reached each new stage of activation.

His heart sank as he realised the machine was less than a quarter of the way to complete operation.

A fit of coughing suddenly seized him, his aching frame shaking. Fine droplets of blood sprayed down onto the white cloth of the arms of his burnoose with each wheezing, rattling cough.

What's wrong with…?

The machine powered quietly into a new phase. The rumbling of machinery from somewhere far below grew a little louder, and a dizzying wave of nausea struck him at the same time.

With a growing sense of horror his keen mind suddenly made the connection. He realised with a hideously clarity that sent stabbing bursts of alarm into his brain that it had all been designed to draw upon the immortal and sustainable life-force of a vampire – in this case, Komashin himself. Jaraxl's own life was draining far too quickly, and at this rate he was not going to have enough energy for him to maintain and control the device through to its final stages. Whatever the machine was doing, whatever processes he had set into motion, it was all going to lose containment with his death - and as a mere mortal, that outcome was clearly assured if he remained linked to it.

Frantically he tried to abort the procedure and power down the machine, but he was unable to shut it off – furthermore, with a frenzied stab of panic, he was unable to extract his hands from within the device. They were locked tightly in place.

In a mad panic he twisted and thrashed against the device, kicked uselessly with his legs, and wrenched his arms back as sharply as he could manage – but all to no avail. He was trapped.

Jaraxl's hysterical cries of terror, and pleading screams for help were drowned out by the heavy walls that surrounded him, and by the rumbling of the machine as it entered a new phase of activation.

As the slow hours crawled by he continued his futile struggle: screaming, kicking, calling out – trying distraughtly to find some method with which he could power down the machine and disengage his trapped arms.

But the machine refused to respond, and a terrible certainty grew in Jaraxl's heart that the machine, once activated, could not be stopped until it had completed its task.

Later, in the unknown stretches of the night, Jaraxl knelt before the device – desperate to take some of the insufferable strain from his aching shoulders – while hopeless sobs racked his failing body. He was beyond fighting now, his throat hoarse from useless screaming and his eyes dry of tears. In the slow hours that crawled past there was nothing to occupy his mind but the machine and the stark horror of his situation, no surcease of the mad panic that swelled and grew within his heart, which now felt like some great steel hand was crushing it. His physical discomfort was increased by the burning need to empty his bladder, and a maddening itch that was worrying his face just above his upper lip. But these concerns seemed trivial when compared to the danger unfolding before him. In his mind, thanks to the strangely symbiotic connection he had forged with the machine, he could see the power levels radically spiking and dropping erratically. Already they were too high, and the methods he had used before to regulate and direct them no longer appeared to be working.

Another low rumble gently shook the room. Another ruby light burst into life at the front of the bronze oval machine, but far too many remained unlit. More copper panels slid open on the walls, and somewhere far below another part of Komashin's device came to life.

Jaraxl closed his eyes, and prayed to Agralis for help.

*

Morning found the dying sun hanging like a fading ember in a sky that was the leaden colour of ash. In the numerous chapels scattered around the city and in the fane of Agralis atop the central ziggurat, long droning prayers were being recited and libations poured as they had since time immemorial – but the gods seemed to have turned away from the people, and the prayers remained unheeded. On the roof of the temple, the last surviving sacred baboons now rose up, trying to warm their bellies on the scant sunlight.

The feeble morning light that filtered in through the heavy grill of the small window set high up in Komashin's main chamber fell upon the weak and dehydrated figure of Jaraxl. He sagged against the side of the machine like a limp doll, his bloodless face was gaunt and pale and his cheeks had already started to sink in upon themselves. His greying hair was dropping out in clumps, and his eyes – now blind and rheumy – stared vacantly ahead as he struggled feebly to release his skeletal hands from the machine. Despite the rapid degeneration of his body, his mind remained hideously aware, but trapped within a steadily failing shell racked with pain and increasing deterioration.

With a grinding whirr the machine entered another new phase – long metal strands were descending swiftly from the walls of the chamber, sparking and glowing with heat. Jaraxl was unable to see this new development, but he could feel the heat and hear the sparks, and the air around him filled with a choking, acrid stench.

The initial vibration in the heart of the device had grown exponentially - a dangerous, out-of-control thrumming that was shattering and splitting the rock around it. It was the sound of an unregulated build-up of power, growling and snarling for release that was denied to it.

But Jaraxl was too weak to maintain control of the device.

From outside the chamber came the dim clamour of voices, and a thumping on the solid metal door announced the presence of unexpected visitors.

"Open this door immediately!" a muffled voice demanded – bearing with it the authority of the City Guards.

The call was followed by a frantic, pained cry in a voice he knew immediately as Salla's: "Don't open it! They're here to stop you!"

Her voice terminated suddenly in a pained howl and a faint sound like a gauntleted hand striking out.

"You've no way out. Open this door and the judges may go easy on you!" the guard resumed, as did the pounding.

But Jaraxl was unable to move. His withered body was merely a dead appendage to his mind, and remained fused with the device. He tried to call out – wanted to beg them to break into the chamber and separate him. Now, even the prospect of death was a welcome release from the life-leeching machine before him. But he had no voice with which to answer, only a faint rasping hiss escaped his cracked lips.

Within his chest a tight band had formed – crushing and constricting, preventing him from drawing breath. His eyes bulged and his body twitched as his heart spasmed. The chamber around him felt like it warped and swayed, spinning before his half-blind eyes like one of the wooden spinning-tops he had played with as a child. His legs flopped weakly, his feet kicking pathetically and ineffectually at the flags on the floor.

There was a final gurgling gasp – foaming spittle flying from his lips – and then his body slumped against the side of Komashin's ancient machine.

As his life ebbed and finally failed, the device went into an unregulated overload.

There was no warning as Komashin's systems went critical.

A wave of invisible energy arced out of the rumbling, shuddering machine, splitting the copper globe asunder and blasting apart the withered corpse that still clung lifelessly to it. The lethal shockwave - the by-product of a dangerously unstable mix of science and sorcery - coursed, roiled and surged outwards in every direction from the machine, detonating the top of Komashin's tower in a violent spray of debris and grit, killing Salla and the guards instantly and casting huge blocks of cracked and charred stone down into the crowded streets below. People screamed and ran, hurling themselves into doorways and taking vain shelter under the market-stalls and archways. But there was no protection from the deadly blast, burning with searing heat and alive with radiation. Like a silent and transparent pyroclastic flow, it burned through the streets and tore walls apart, vaporising all organic matter before it.

In the end, it was the cataclysm of legend. The kind of disaster that would be on the tongues of men and women for thousands of years, and which may even have been attributed as an act of the vengeful gods - that is, had any survived to carry on the tales. But Komashin's powers as both a scientist and a sorcerer had been enormous, and, accidentally misused, those unleashed powers were awesome and horrifying to behold. The terrible shockwave didn't stop with the city. It drove on – rippling across the countryside, through the frozen mountains, across the iced lakes and oceans – bringing destruction and consuming life where it found it, until the whole planet was enveloped in its invisible and lethal shroud.

In the silent ruins of Wevven, the shattered buttresses, collapsed ramparts and fractured, leaning edifices reared their splintered forms skyward, transformed in cataclysmic seconds from structures of daily life into colossal and frost-covered tombstones of an extinct civilization.

Whilst overhead, the sun they had been so desperate to save, outlived them all.

Touch of Silence

    Kara slipped unseen through the darkness of the alley, clinging to the deeper shadows and the obscuring veils of steam that rose into the night from the vents near the gutters. Around her the buildings shivered almost imperceptibly at her approach, a movement too subtle for most to notice, yet still she held her breath. Her target was bio-sensitive, as she was. She knew that he could read and sense the changing bioelectric patterns of life forms that most were blind to, and that made him both rare and dangerous. Closing her eyes, she pressed her hands against the walls, whispering softly to them. She could feel every one of the fine veins that ran across their surface beneath her fingers, and sensed the soft pulse of their beating hearts

– and as she whispered to them, she felt the structures become calm and relaxed.

They were not her target, nor were they in her way. They had nothing to fear.

Kara had always been able to *project*. It was a gift found in only a small percentage of the population, and it was her secret, known only to her employer. It aided her well in her contracts, allowing her to project her will, feelings and emotions into other life-forms through physical contact, influencing and manipulating according to her desires. The only beings immune to the process were the others who bore the same gift, but it was rare in humans, found only in those that had some Daissh parentage somewhere in their ancestry. But a past mistake that had nearly cost her own life had taught her not to dismiss the possibility in *any* of her targets, no matter how remote the chances might be.

She hugged the wall as she reached the end of the alley, invisible in the shadows as she studied the street. He had come this way. She smelled his cheap aftershave on the night air, mixed with sweat – he was nervous, afraid. He knew he was being hunted.

Something moved behind her and her muscles tensed instinctively, one hand silently snatching the pistol from the holster at her side. The gun was drawn even before she had finished turning.

From out of a nearby cluster of recycling bins a small dark creature had scurried into sight, looking like a curious cross between a pill bug and a scorpion. Instantly she lowered her weapon with a sigh. It was only a Dar'het. She holstered her gun back out of sight under her jacket and scowled as the small animal scuttled past, moving to the next set of bins. She hated them. Not only did they look revolting, but they were totally outside her ability to sense. The Daissh had introduced them to the planet decades ago. Small life-forms engineered to consume most forms of waste matter and convert them safely into a nutrient-rich biomatter. They were the ultimate recyclers.

Turning her focus back to the task at hand she crossed the street with a catlike grace, moving just slowly enough to avoid raising suspicion and just quickly enough to limit the amount of time she was out in the open to less than twelve seconds. On the other side, veiled again in shadow, Kara closed her eyes and joined her consciousness to the closest structure. The wall shuddered as her mind engaged it, and then spoke, whispering to her with its alien thoughts. It had taken her over a year to begin to understand the strange language of the alien biotech, but she had long grown used to it. The man she sought had come this way less than a minute before. The building clearly remembered him passing by, half walking and half running, smelling strongly of fear and glancing over his shoulder with unusual frequency.

Kara silently thanked the structure as she disengaged from it, feeling once more the curious sense of momentary dislocation that always came when her consciousness had bonded to, and then parted, from another. Even after all these years, it was a sensation that she had never quite been able to get used to.

She still remembered the first time she had linked with the mind of a Daissh structure – it had been so alien to the minds she was used to experiencing that she'd screamed aloud as their consciousnesses had touched. It had been like walking blind into a twisting darkened room of strange angles and shapes, not knowing what was floor or wall or ceiling, while lights, sounds and impulses and sensations that she had no means of processing or understanding had howled around her like a wild storm, disorientating and frightening.

It was Schaefer that had truly helped her find her potential, along with the means and opportunity to embrace her gifts fully. She had been working as a hooker at the time. It had been easy money, at least the way she did things. It simply took a hand placed onto theirs to convince them they'd had their money's worth, and it meant she could avoid actually sleeping with any of them. They sickened her – lustful, obese middle aged fools desperate to get their greedily groping hands on anything young and nubile. She enjoyed watching them hand over their money for nothing but flushed faces and false memories. But she had allowed herself to get complacent, too cocky and self-assured in the game she was playing, and one of her clients had surprised her. He must have had a trace of Daissh blood somewhere in his lineage, because suddenly the trick wasn't working, her manipulations fell flat, and he started to get rough – angry at her sudden reticence to play along as promised. He had forced himself upon her and in a panic she killed him, smashed a metal lamp down over his head, and it amazed her how easy it had been, and how much satisfaction she had watching one of the very people she had spent her life despising fall at her feet.

It wasn't long afterwards that Schaefer had found her, recognising her unique talents, and her new life had started, working for him and his associates.

As she set off down the street once more, she again caught the now familiar scent of her target's aftershave on the evening air, and quickened her progress. Around her humans and Daissh bustled past, but most of them were too wrapped up in their own private worlds to even notice each other, let alone her. It was always the way in the cities: the bigger the communities the more alone the inhabitants were. But at least the air was clear and fresh and pleasant, if a little chilly with the steady approach of winter. Soon the Daissh would cover the city with heat membranes, and winter would be left outside. But by then Kara hoped to be out of the city and back on one of the ocean-bed colonies, most likely Iowaen. It was the place where she had been born, and the only place she ever felt any sense of peace or belonging – down in the deep, with the cold dark oceans pressing in all around them and bioluminescent coral lighting the streets with a soft blue-green light. But she would miss the freshness of the natural breeze. It was one of the few things about this world that she loved.

Then she saw him, a small middle aged man in a crumpled suit, and her senses and thoughts instantly honed in on her target. He was running up to one of the buildings, face flushed, checking his watch anxiously as he reached for the door. In his haste he nearly fumbled, almost dropped his briefcase, and then his fingers swept the organic sensors and the building immediately responded to his DNA. The doors opened and he darted inside, desperately seeking shelter within as the membranes on the door folded shut behind him

She moved swiftly up to the door, allowing herself a small smile.

I have you now.

Kara reached for the sensor, but instead of sweeping her hand past it she pressed her fingers against it, merging her mind effortlessly with the structure. The structural biotech that the Daissh had brought with them to the Earth was extremely susceptible to her gifts. It was the fatal flaw they had never been able to breed out, and because of that she knew no doors or walls would keep her from reaching him. His sanctuary had become his tomb.

She slipped inside before the doors had even finished opening.

There was a Daissh and a human inside, both behind a small security counter. The human looked to be in his early thirties and wore the black uniform of a security officer, but the Daissh wore the traditional D'nul garb of the worker caste, and was clearly monitoring the biorhythms of the building as part of routine maintenance. At the sight of her the security guard stood, a frown creasing his face, and Kara realised at once that he was obviously familiar with each of the tenants here. The Daissh, aware something had changed in the emotional atmosphere of the room turned, eyes blinking and probosces twitching as she sensed the air.

Without breaking her stride Kara moved toward the desk, allowing a friendly smile to fill her lips. She knew she was desirable, she could feel it every time a man's gaze rested on her just that little bit longer than it should, and she could feel it now.

"I was hoping you can help me," she said, deepening her smile. He was interested, she could tell. He hadn't reached for his radio or his gun, and his stance clearly showed his guard was down, even given his surprise at her entrance. She could use all that to her advantage.

"This is a private building. How did you…?" he asked as he moved toward her, but mid sentence his gaze dropped – just for a second - to the outline of her breasts, and she felt a ripple of arousal radiate from him.

But his distraction had allowed her to get close enough.

In a single fluid motion she lunged for him. Instinctively he stepped back, reaching for his gun, but she grabbed his arm and twisted it sharply away with her left hand, even as her right drew the ceremonial D'kis blade from out of her belt – the organic blade hardening to a razor point in a microsecond. She drove it into his heart and he died instantly, crumpling to the floor at her feet like a puppet whose strings had been severed.

She doubted whether that had been the kind of penetration he had wanted to share with her, but she pushed it instantly from her mind. She didn't have time for games when there was a contract at stake. Later, when the job was done and she'd retired to the quiet seclusion of one of the many mixed-sex brothels that littered the southern quarter of the city, she would allow herself to relax and share some fun and pleasure with another human being; at least, for a time.

The Daissh had backed up against the wall, shrilling in terror, probosces twitching frantically, but she had made no attempt to escape. For a second Kara wondered why – and then saw that two of her probosces were still engaged with the building for the maintenance check. The Daissh couldn't disengage without causing herself a fatal injury.

Before Kara slit the Daissh's frontal air sac, she allowed her to catch a glimpse of the D'kis blade, and saw the flash of outrage that flickered alongside the terror in those black eyes. The D'kis was a sacred blade to the Daissh – used only to cut the cord at each new birth, and one that they never used to take or harm a life. To use the blade – itself a living thing – in such a way, was to them the ultimate profanity.

Doesn't stop it from being one of the best damn weapons around though, Kara smiled to herself as she sheathed the blade back into her belt. To use it for anything else was just a waste.

She reached across the security desk, her fingers resting on the controls as she sought to make a connection with the building. Instead a wall of panic and fear, so sudden and overwhelming it nearly sent her reeling, slammed into her. It took her a moment to shake off the effects, and she cursed herself for the slip. The Daissh she had killed had still been linked with the building at the moment of death, the structure had seen and felt it all and now was terrified and going into a wild, blind panic. She would get nothing from it for hours now.

Fine. I'll do this the hard way, she mused angrily as she approached the wall terminal where the Daissh had been connected. One of the Daissh's slender probosces was still engaged, and she tore it free with a glare of annoyance, before pressing her hand across the port. The building shrieked again, and she could feel its mind recoiling from her touch, the death screams of the Daissh still ringing through its awareness, but she ignored it, focusing instead on the subtle traces of the other life-forms that were contained within it. It took a few seconds for her to feel beyond the pulsing waves of fear that the building was sending out. Then she felt them, faint, like half-glimpsed ghosts or a whisper in a crowded room, and she focused on them one at a time: the couple, huddled romantically together on the second floor; the lonely old man lost in regrets on the third; the family contentedly finishing up supper on the sixth. And then she felt the stark fear and the terror of the man alone up on the seventh floor, the desperate and frantic panic of someone who knows he is being hunted.

Seventh it is, she smiled, slipping from the lobby and up the stairs without making a sound.

The seventh floor was quiet and dimly-lit, the hallway stretching off to the left and right from the top of the stairs, but she went left, sensing her quarry more strongly now she was closer to him. The building was still screaming, ringing in her mind, but she pushed it from her thoughts as best she could. She wondered if her target could sense it as well. Would he now know she was in the building? Or would he still believe he had found a measure of sanctuary within these walls?

She stopped outside the door that she knew to be his, and pressed her hand lightly against it. But there was no way of persuading the structure to open the door in its agitated state, so she unsheathed the D'kis and slipped the micro-fine blade into the entry panel interface, closing her eyes as she tried to sense and cut the specific nerve-fibres that were linked to door access. The building shrieked anew as the razor-sharp blade slashed through sinew and nerves one after another, and the lights in the hallway flickered uncontrollably.

From inside the room she sensed an increase in the level of fear from her target.

He knew she was here now.

With a final slash of the D'kis the building howled in silent agony that only she could sense, and the door sagged inward like a severed muscle.

The room beyond was pitch black.

Kara tensed and stepped back away from the door, puzzled and confused. She could no longer sense the occupant inside, and she should have been able to – even over the wailing and screaming now flooding her senses from the walls around her, there should have been something.

For a second a feeling akin to fear blossomed in her own heart, but she pushed it away. Whatever he had done, he wasn't going to be able to hide from her for long.

She drove the D'kis back into the access panel, twisting and slashing at the fibres and tendons within. Overhead the light in the hallway fizzled out as the blood-flow to it was severed. Thick green-brown blood, more like a dense soup, was spattering down the walls from the ravaged access panel. The screaming from the structure had risen to a mad, keening wail, and the walls themselves seemed to shiver from pain and shock.

Kara felt no remorse for her actions. It was just a building, and they hardly had any kind of existence to speak of. All she cared about now was getting her kill and then getting paid. This job had already taken far too long and had stopped being fun.

With the darkness in the hallway equal to that within the apartment, she slipped silently in, listening to the room around her.

He was still here, somewhere. He had to be. There was no other way out, and if he had opened or broken a window membrane she would have known about it.

So why can't I sense you anymore? She frowned, unwilling to admit to the shiver of unease the thought brought her. She didn't like not being in control of the chase. Something was very wrong here.

She pressed a hand softly against the skin beside her eye, activating her vision membrane – another one of the technological gifts the Daissh had brought with them, designed for sensing illness within their living structures, at least until the technology had got onto the black market when its other uses had been realised. As the organic filters slid across her eyeballs the room around her burst into a dazzling aura of colour, and she pressed the membrane control twice quickly, filtering out the life-signals from the surrounding structure.

But as she did, her blood ran cold.

The room around her was alive with movement – the walls, ceiling, even the floor, were all pulsing with dozens of separate small bio-signatures. They were scurrying quickly toward her like moths to a flame. In a heartbeat she recognised their body shape as Dar'hets – and her frown deepened, for Dar'hets rarely came inside structures, in fact they were generally programmed to avoid entering them except in emergencies.

All too late she saw the nearest one raise its tail, and a tiny projectile embedded itself in her neck. Terrified and confused she staggered backwards, reeling and stumbling as she half-stepped and half-fell into the hallway. Her hand was at her neck in an instant, pulling the bone-like dart free, but she could already feel that it had done its work. Her vision was blurring and a hot burning sensation was spreading up her neck, constricting her throat. She took one step, two. She tried for a third, but then fell, landing heavily on the thinly carpeted hallway. She struggled to raise her head to look back, but it felt like a lead weight on her neck, and her eyes refused to stay open.

Dimly she saw the feet that had moved to stand next to her head outlined by their own body heat, but by now she was sinking, falling, spiralling down into a deep black abyss, leaving her physical form far behind.

*

"Dar'hets are fascinating creatures, aren't they?" a voice said softly.

Kara's eyes opened painfully to a view of the floor, out of focus. Her head span drunkenly and her throat was dry and scratchy. Her arms and shoulders ached with a dull, hollow throb. It took a few seconds for everything to come grudgingly into place, and she blinked blearily, trying to swallow as she lifted her head with a wince.

She was restrained in a chair, her body tied with some kind of cord and her wrists bound to the arms of the chair. There was no gag in her mouth, but when she tried to speak no sound came out.

"They're harmless, of course," the voice continued, from somewhere off to her right, "at least as the Daissh bio-engineer them. But you'd be amazed at how easily a few small tweaks in the right places can remedy that."

Kara swallowed, and tried to speak again. A faint hoarse croak was her only success.

"The sting has paralysed your vocal chords," the voice answered. "It will wear off in time, though perhaps not fast enough for you."

The figure was moving now, coming around the side of the chair. She turned her head, as much as her stiff and protesting neck would permit, and saw the face of the man she had been hunting smiling back at her. He no longer looked like the same scared target she had been pursuing; in fact, she sensed nothing from him now but prideful satisfaction.

"A specially tailored epinephrine patch," he said, as if sensing her thoughts, "coupled with a good run. Helps to simulate all the sensations of fear you would have been expecting to sense."

A flicker of realisation dawned within her, and she sat up, straining against her bonds, as her eyes widened.

"Yes, I can see you've worked it out," he laughed gently. "Your employers sent me. They have decided that you have become too dangerous. You know too much, and are too hard to control. In short, you've become a liability. A problem."

Another croak escaped her lips, a futile gesture at defiant bravado as she fought against the flexing bonds that now bit deeply into her wrists.

"I am here to solve that problem."

Her eyes locked on his now, filled with terror.

"Yes," he smiled. "You were never the hunter this night."

She fell silent, but her eyes now darted to the corners of the room, seeking some means of escape, some detail she could use to her advantage.

"But I'm not going to kill you."

She snapped her gaze back on him, puzzled, suspicious.

"I don't take lives," he said. "That's your job. Instead, I will simply drain you of who you are. But you will live, in a manner of speaking. I'm even told it can be quite peaceful, like going to sleep."

She struggled and squirmed now, terror widening her eyes and quickening her heart. She could see that he could sense it all, just as she had with so many victims before.

"You see, you bring the touch of death," he said, as he pressed his fingers to her skin – one hand resting on her arm, the other just above her eyes. "A gift you have given to so many, with barely a passing thought."

She could feel his consciousness flowing into hers now.

"Instead, I have another gift. I bring the touch of silence."

A constricting darkness swarmed through her; like a raging torrent of surging water, downing all that she knew and all that she was. She fought with all her will to hold on – but the darkness kept coming, and she couldn't turn it back.

It unravelled within her, like a big ball of yarn into which her life was wound – her name, her life, her identity, even her hopes and fears and desires. Everything that she clung to and called a part of her, it was all being stripped away, consumed by the spreading void of darkness that was blossoming in her mind like a lethal flower.

In a panic she recoiled backwards in the chair, almost tipping it, the bonds around her wrists cutting into flesh hard enough to draw blood.

"The ancient Greeks spoke of the waters of Lethe, the river of oblivion," a voice whispered, though she could no longer quite remember to whom it belonged. "Drink deep, and forget."

She dug her nails into the arm of the chair, her teeth gritted.

Her mother's face flickered before her bright and sharp – the only brief memory she had of her, and then faded like a dream. The names and faces of lovers, short-lived liaisons that never went deeper than the physical, and past contracts that she had neutralised all came and went with impossible speed, sinking rapidly into the darkness that swallowed them greedily like thick tar. She grabbed for them, tried to snatch and hold each memory in her mind, but it was like trying to grab a ghost – there was nothing to latch onto, for they had already started vanishing even as she looked at them. Memories of a young life alone on the streets after the death of her parents – running from foster homes and the police, the cold nights and the dark shadows, a life spent learning to envy and despise those around her, and then it was gone too.

Schaefer's face flickered before her now. A final vivid memory of the last time they had spoken in the dimly-lit privacy of his office, a room that resonated with the ghosts of the secrets, lies and lives that had been decided there. His face was red and angry, and there was something deeper in his eyes – fear.

"I'm the best you have, and you know it," she said, and she knew from the look on his face that he knew it too. "You need me. And I want a bigger cut, or I'm out."

"Don't flatter yourself," Schaefer said, but the fear stayed in his eyes and the mask of strength with which he tried to cover it failed to fool her. She wondered how she had ever once thought him impressive and powerful. "You're in no position to demand anything."

"After all the messes I've cleared up for you and your associates these past four years? After all the dirty little secrets I've swept under the rug at your request? What I know could ruin you."

Schaefer stayed back behind his desk, as always he made sure never to let her close enough to touch him. "Be careful who you threaten," he warned.

She slipped her hand down to her side, letting him catch a glimpse of the gun at her belt. "I could say the same, and we both know I'm the better shot. Faster too."

"You're a shadow. One that wouldn't be missed."

"That may have worked in the past," she said, cocky and self-assured, "but I'm wiser now, and not so easily scared. You know what I'm capable of better than most. You should, you helped me discover the depths of my talents."

"If you try this, my associates will come down on you. I won't be able to protect you."

"As if I need anyone's protection."

Then the memory fractured, splintering into shards like broken glass, and the void claimed it - just another lost fragment of identity swirling into oblivion.

"It will all be over soon."

She could no longer remember where she was, or what was happening to her. She knew she was in danger, but not why. She thought she remembered that someone else was with her – she had just heard a voice, hadn't she?

Then that too was gone.

She would have screamed, but her throat was still paralysed and only a hoarse choked wheeze escaped into the room.

It was the last sound she would never remember hearing.

The darkness became total; became everything.

"Sleep now," he said softly, even knowing she couldn't understand him.

A short time later a man quietly stepped out into the hallway of an apartment building and slipped away into the shadows of the world. The name against which the apartment had been leased was not his own, and nobody in the building saw him again after that night. Even his DNA log was gone from the building's memory.

He left behind one resolved problem and many unanswered questions: two murdered bodies in the lobby, a room full of poisoned Dar'hets, and an empty shell with a human face; a shell that breathed and blinked and aged, but which was utterly devoid of any form of awareness or self. A shell that never moved or spoke, laughed or cried, and that had to be fed intravenously right up until the day she died peacefully in her sleep.

A body truly touched by silence.

The Fourth Setting

Henders had that look in his eye, the one that always meant trouble. He had been pacing restlessly around the lab for the last half hour, ever since that curious envelope had arrived, and now he looked both agitated and excited in equal measure. A thin line of sweat beaded his creased brow beneath his swiftly receding hairline, and his upper lip was almost quivering. His gaze flicked nervously to the curious squat pillar of grey-green stone that sat amidst a sea of wires, cables and softly-humming monitoring devices; a stone that had been the sole consuming object of both his time and attention for weeks now.

"We're going to try the fourth setting," he announced in the tone of voice he always used for decisions that were not to be questioned.

From where he sat on the other side of the lab Tom McKenzie watched him uneasily as he flicked through the results from their earlier tests. He doubted that Henders had been eating or sleeping properly for days now – maybe even weeks judging by the bags under his eyes, the gauntness that had crept into his face, and the speed with which his frayed temper had been giving out, but he knew that no amount of argument on his part would do any good. The man could teach mules how to be stubborn.

"It's late," McKenzie commented, though he made no attempt to check his watch. Such a gesture was likely only to anger Henders and make him even more unreasonable. "We're the only ones still here. Shouldn't we wait until we have a full team back in tomorrow?"

"Science doesn't sleep."

"No, but people do."

"We're close, McKenzie – close to understanding this ancient marvel that sits among us. I thought that you of all people would share in that passion, that dedication."

"I do – and I understand, this is important." McKenzie ventured tactfully. "But I've got a wife and a two-year old kid at home. I've got to think of them as well."

"You are. With the work we're doing here, you're putting food on their table and paying off that new television set, and you're also helping make their world a safer place. And tonight, while they sleep soundly, you and I are going to try the fourth setting."

"We got those bad power spikes on the third setting – dangerous ones, remember?" he reminded Henders cautiously. "With the levels of energy that rock is emitting, who knows what might happen?"

"What's your point?" Henders narrowed his eyes as he shot a fierce glare at McKenzie.

"Have I really got to spell it out?"

"If you have concerns or doubts, then enlighten me," Henders said testily.

"This rock defies everything we know. Not only is it a mystery to every geologist we've consulted, it also appears to be *generating* energy, and seems to respond to us by increasing its output to levels that shouldn't be possible. Yet it's not magnetic or radioactive, has no surface temperature, and as far as we can determine there are no discernable electrostatic charges present within it at all. Nothing that should allow it to do what it has been doing. I just think we should stop and go over the findings very thoroughly before-"

Henders shot him a look that could have melted steel, furious that anyone dared question his decision. "Caution is for those who have time."

"With all due respect, we've all the time in the world."

"Is that so?" Henders folded his arms, his gaze icy. "What if this isn't the only stone of its kind out there? We were lucky that a US archaeological team found this first and not a Russian one. Can you imagine if this got into the hands of the Commies? They've already started firing rockets and dogs into space – just think what they could do with a source of power like this!"

McKenzie fell silent and let his eyes return to the sheaf of papers he had been studying. He knew Henders had a point - the application for the rock went far beyond a potential source of limitless renewable energy. It would undoubtedly have endless applications for weapons technology too. His gaze shifted to the manila envelope still sitting on the next desk, the one with the government stamp on the front and Henders' name in thick black print right under that, and he wondered for the hundredth time just what was in it. It had been hand-delivered that afternoon by a man in a dark suit that McKenzie had never seen around the labs before. But he recognised the stern unsmiling face of a government official when he saw one, and that's exactly what he had seen staring out from under the stranger's pristine black fedora. There was more going on here than Henders was telling, that much was certain, but McKenzie knew better than to try and press for information before Henders was ready to reveal it.

He just wished he knew more about the location where the rock had been discovered – supposedly some isolated little island somewhere in the South Pacific Ocean. Word on the grapevine was that the local tribe apparently venerated the rock, claiming it had prophetic properties – supposedly giving glimpses of other worlds, places and times, and allowed them to commune in a dream-trance with their strange gods, all in return for blood offerings made atop the stone. There were wild tales of victims apparently flayed alive or garrotted while shamans with pierced faces carved bloody chunks out of them with a flint blade, before dressing in skinned strips of dripping flesh and dancing into a wild frenzy to the damnable pounding of tribal drums. And all that, allegedly, while the rest of the village chanted and screamed, as they cavorted and danced in a wild throng around the sacrificial stone. It sounded beyond barbaric, and were customs utterly unlike any found on the wholly peaceful neighbouring islands. Just the thought of it was enough to churn McKenzie's stomach. He had even heard claims that three of the expedition members had actually been slain just trying to smuggle the stone back to their boat. It was hard to believe things like that still happened now in 1959 – it sounded more like something out of the dark ages.

"McKenzie?"

He blinked and realised he'd been drifting in thought – worse, he'd been staring right at the envelope. He looked up, face flushing. "Yes?"

"I said can you activate the electrical field?" Henders repeated again. If he had noticed McKenzie's interest in the envelope he gave no sign. "I'll monitor responses and calibrate from the second station."

"I want my objections noted," McKenzie said as he made his way over to the generator controls. Henders gave an irritable nod and wave of the hand, but McKenzie knew he was unlikely to actually bother noting down anything. With a silent sigh he seated himself before the console and activated the switch, taking the dial up to the midway point before the first setting. He could feel the familiar tingle as the electricity flowed through the rock and watched as already the readout dials were showing triple what they should have been.

"Increase up to two," Henders called over.

"We need to cycle up slowly," McKenzie warned, "we have to give the equipment time to…"

"Increase to two," the order came again, the tone less pleasant.

"Increasing now," McKenzie muttered, shaking his head. There was a noticeable dip in the ceiling lights as the dial turned and more electricity was channelled through the stone. The needles were now spiking and dancing dangerously high, and McKenzie recalled the first time they had dared take the setting to this level and the alarm that had created among the lab staff – back then, only just a few weeks ago, the thought of doing what they planned to try tonight would have been unthinkable.

"Now proceed to three."

McKenzie opened his mouth to protest then closed it again, knowing it would fall on deaf ears. He twisted the dial all the way to three, his body tensing. Around them the air was filled with the crackle and spark of electricity, the background hiss of static and the hum of the machines as they drew on more and more power. A smell of heating solder and ozone assaulted their nostrils – along with a foul stench like burning rubber that was growing stronger by the second. Henders meanwhile stood like a statue, his gaze fixed intently on the dials before him, mouth parted just a fraction, and that obsessive twinkle sparkling in his eyes that reminded McKenzie of the look of a kid coming down to open the gifts around the tree on Christmas morning.

"We're at three now," McKenzie reported, casting a worried glance at the readings that were coming back in. "This doesn't look good."

"Understood. Hold it here for a second."

The lights fizzled and dipped overhead, and the burning smell was getting worse – more acrid. The dials on the console continued to spike, but hadn't gone into the red yet. Even so, McKenzie felt an uneasy feeling in his gut and wiped his sweating palms on his legs.

"Get ready to take it up to the fourth setting," Henders gestured excitedly, his hand trembling.

"Have you seen these readings?" McKenzie called over, "they look worse than last time."

"Everything's fine. I expected this."

"Seriously?"

"It's fine."

"We're about to blow half the equipment in here if we don't give it time to adjust. And even if we do, at these levels…"

"I reinforced the capacitors myself – they can take it."

"This is crazy – you'll get us both killed!"

"We must keep going. The key to unlocking the potential within the rock lies with the correct application of channelled energy. It is my belief we are dealing with more than a mere power source here, rather something created by a science yet unknown to us – but for what purpose? What reason?" he stared over at the stone, a half-smile crossing his face. "We shall soon discover its purpose. I know we are close to finding the truth."

"How can you know that? That's not science, that's conjecture."

"Educated conjecture based upon the evidence gathered so far," Henders said, waving the accusation away.

"So let's gather more – slowly, under more controlled conditions. Why are we rushing in like workmen with a sledgehammer? Science requires a finely-tuned and careful approach. You know that – or you used to. What's changed?"

"Time is of the essence."

"Why?" McKenzie demanded furiously. "Why all the sudden urgency to figure out this thing? What aren't you telling me?"

"Because-!" Henders snarled, then visibly reigned himself in before continuing, "there *is* another stone. The Russians have it."

McKenzie fell back onto his seat, all the arguments and warnings that had been about to leave his lips had fallen silent.

"Now you understand," Henders ran a shaking hand through his thin greying hair. "The government wants to know what we have here, and we're lucky they are letting us work on it. If we fail to get results, they'll take it to someone who can – our funding with it. But worse than that, if the maximum power output of this rock is even close to what I think it may be, then in the hands of the Russians – well, we won't stand a chance unless we possess that power too, or can unlock its secrets first. If we don't beat them to understanding what we have here, it could be the end of us all."

"I didn't know," McKenzie said softly, shaking his head.

"You weren't supposed to. Now you do. And I promise you, the Commies won't stop or worry about safety concerns. They'll do what it takes to unlock the secrets of that rock – and harness the true strength of its power. Now you see why we must press on?"

McKenzie nodded slowly, humbled and stunned. He reached for the dial, feeling the cold steel under the tips of his fingers as he swallowed dryly. "Ready for the fourth setting."

"We're making history tonight," Henders declared. "I know it."

With that, McKenzie turned the dial.

The needles spiked and flickered as the power output increased dramatically. The stone was spitting out energy levels at a rate even greater than either of them had expected or thought possible. A shrill whine rose up over the rumbling of the capacitors as they struggled to deal with the increase and the acrid smell was becoming unbearable. McKenzie was sure something must be burning back inside one of the units. Sweat coursed down his face as the machines continued to heat up.

The squat pillar of rock sitting amidst the coils of wire gave no visible sign of the power that was now rippling out of it, invisible and incredible, and McKenzie found his gaze moving back to it, a mix of curiosity and awe filling him. But there was something else too – something more primal. It had taken him a few nights to work out what it was, it was so deeply buried in his subconscious, but now he understood. There was an unaccountable sense of dread and revulsion hanging about that stone – one that went beyond the violent and bloody past connected to it from the sacrifices. It was as though something in the core of his being wanted to recoil from it and run screaming from the room, or to tip it into the biggest pit he could find and shovel dirt onto it, to bury it from the world. He never would have said anything about this to Henders. He knew the old man would berate him for giving into foolish superstition and weak emotional fears, but still, there was something about that rock that was *wrong*, and on some instinctive level, he knew it. It was as if he could hear the tribal drums every time he looked at it, could see blood running down the rock and taste the coppery taint thickly in the air. And behind those drums and the shrill wailing of the wildly thrashing and dancing natives, behind all that blood and chaos and carnage… he could hear whispers, faint and unnerving, coming out of that rock. And the harder he strained, the more he leaned forward, heart hammering in his chest as he tried to listen to what those strange voices were saying, the more he thought they weren't really voices at all, at least not human ones.

A capacitor sparked and failed, snapping McKenzie's attention back onto his readouts. Everything was pushing into the red, and if Henders had not overridden the safety shut-offs the night before, the systems would have deactivated automatically by now.

"This is too much," McKenzie warned. "We should power it back down and go over the readings we got tonight."

"Just a few seconds more!"

"I don't think the equipment will-"

As if finishing his sentence for him a spark burst out of the side of one of the consoles followed by a cloud of thick noxious smoke. McKenzie scrabbled for the nearest extinguisher and doused the now dead unit in dry powder. The other machines were also showing signs of succumbing to the overwhelming stress on their systems. Warning lights flashed and flickered and fans whirred as they struggled to cool the failing equipment.

"Recalibrate!" Henders screamed, his eyes wide as he watched the output register. "Look at it – look! The power levels are accelerating faster! These readings, they are truly-"

But that was the last thing McKenzie heard before the lab exploded.

The force of the blast lifted him up and slammed him backwards, catapulting him across a bench in a spray of heat, sparks and broken glass. He landed heavily, gasping as the air was punched from his lungs, ears ringing and his whole body dazed and shaking. For a second he couldn't move – only lie stunned and blinking as the room around him shook.

When his world finally settled he eased himself up slowly, his head spinning and the coppery taste of blood flooding his mouth. His shirt had torn open at both elbows and one whole side of his body was screaming at him where he had landed on broken glass. As he sat up he realised he was missing a shoe. His shocked brain tried to work out had happened, but everything was blurry. He blinked twice as he forced himself to stand shakily, then a wave of terror washed over him as his eyesight and mind came back into focus together.

Henders stood in the centre of the room, his body swaying as though he were drunk, the tattered and bloody remains of his lab coat fluttering out around him like ragged streamers. He might simply have been in shock, but McKenzie could see the tendrils that were now coming out of the pillar of rock – translucent stalks that coiled and flexed like flickering tentacles, but which were neither light, nor radiation, nor electricity, but some strange combination of all of these and more – and which had now attached themselves to the back of Henders' head like the strings on a puppet.

"Hellooooooo baby!" the Big Bopper crooned as the radio on the shelf across the lab sputtered and kicked into life. There was one of the strange electrical tendrils coiling about it too, and crazily McKenzie found himself starting to laugh, a shrill high-pitched wail as his nails dug into his palms.

"...Celebrating yesterday's Stanley cup victory by the Montreal Canadiens against the Boston Bruins in..." the radio announced randomly as it skipped through stations, before suddenly falling silent as it shorted out. The ghostly tentacle that had been running across it was now moving up the wall, exploring blindly.

Henders meanwhile was lurching and shambling across the floor like some badly controlled marionette, those tendrils flowing out behind him, writhing and crackling, even as his body began to scorch and wither, his skin visibly darkening as angry red welts erupted across it. The stench that filled the air reminded McKenzie crazily of the family barbecue he had attended just last week and he gagged.

"N'gal thul'sath!" Henders screamed, his voice breaking under the effort and the tendons in his neck sticking out like metal cables. He crashed clumsily against a bench, the flesh on his face melting like hot wax as his hair burst into flame. "Yugg'gai n'ashanna vor y'gth tok'l grrrraaa..."

His scorched fingers groped awkwardly at the scattered objects on the bench – pawing at toppled Bunsen burners and tripods and running unfeelingly through broken glass that tore at the skin. It appeared that he was trying to examine or pick them up, but had forgotten how his hands worked.

"Yugg'gai n'vor ztsdrah Iukkoth d'zzkl…" he howled as he went.

His contorted face was still screaming that insane gibberish moments later when his eyes burst like exploding eggs. He slumped forward, toppling to the floor as the flames raced over his arms and legs before finally consuming him. The tendrils that had been connected with his head broke loose, writhing in the air like agitated serpents.

It took McKenzie a good ten seconds to break through the paralysis of shock that held him rooted to the spot, staring at the blazing remains that lay crumpled just a few feet before him. But the smoke that was filling the air and the searing heat from the wrecked equipment soon jarred him back, and he dropped low to the ground, seeking breathable air, as he crawled painfully toward where he knew the nearest extinguisher would be. The floor was strewn with broken glass and debris and the air overhead was swiftly filling with noxious fumes. Even down close to the floor McKenzie found himself coughing and blinking back tears as his eyes stung and his lungs encountered the toxic smoke. He fumbled almost blindly past the main bench and then his fingers found the wall and stretched up into the haze until they encountered the cold metal of an extinguisher.

He snatched it down, angled the nozzle, then stood and frantically aimed it at the heart of the glow, holding his breath and blinking to try and focus his blurred vision. His eyes already felt like they were being peeled in their sockets, his cheeks were wet with tears and his lungs were now burning with the need to breathe. The kick from the extinguisher took him by surprise and he almost dropped it on his foot. As the cold blast of powder burst forth and doused the flaming equipment the roar it made deafened him. He turned quickly, trying to cover all of the flames, including the still-burning remains of Henders, when the whole extinguisher was ripped from his grip and lifted up into the air. He took a startled step back, colliding with a lab stool, and looked up. Through the swirling haze of fumes and smoke, one of the strange tendrils flexed and moved. He had almost forgotten about them in the panic. It had scooped up the extinguisher and was now examining it, turning it this way and that, almost like a child examining a new toy. Then it hurled the extinguisher aside and McKenzie threw himself to the floor as it tore through the air where his head had been moments before. He sat up, coughing and gasping, and that was when he finally noticed what was happening to the pillar of rock they had been studying. One of the machines had survived the explosion and was still channelling power into it, and whole sections of the pillar liquefied in response – flowing down onto the floor in a molten state and pooling around the base. In the newly exposed sections were curious nubs of grey crystal and strange grooves, shaped in regular clusters of three, around each nub. But what caught his gaze most of all was the unaccountable mass of pale fleshy material that appeared to be pulsing like some kind of obscene heart in the centre of that slab of stone.

Then a sharp tingle, like pins and needles, ran along his leg as a tendril closed around his ankle. The hairs on his whole body stood on end as a strange electrical charge flowed through him. He tried to snatch his leg away, but the tendril coiled up further, wrapping around his calf and tightening painfully around his thigh. A cry of alarm escaped him as he kicked and thrashed, trying to free his trapped limb – but the ghostly tentacle was lifting up now, carrying him with it. Desperately he grabbed at the corner of one of the lab benches, anchoring himself, but his legs were being pulled closer to the pillar and it was taking all of his strength to hold on and keep the rest of him from following along with them.

Flexing translucent feelers were now emerging from the ends of each of the exposed crystal nubs on the pillar, reminding McKenzie of some sea anemones he had once observed, and he watched with growing panic as they gently probed his feet and ankles, running across the smooth leather of his shoe and the torn cloth of his trouser leg. Then one of them penetrated that thin layer of material and sank into his flesh. The pain lanced white-hot through his body and his arms and limbs convulsed painfully, his eyes bulged wildly in their sockets and his teeth clamped together. He couldn't scream, couldn't move, and the agony burned through him even as more of those flexing feelers penetrated his skin and flowed up through his body, running underneath the flesh like spreading varicose veins.

The last remaining machine still channelling power now shorted out as the energy levels overwhelmed it. Thick black smoke belched from the side of the damaged console in plumes – and the warning glow of flames flared through the metal grating on the side as an electrical fire broke out.

But McKenzie was oblivious to the flames taking hold just a few feet from him. He was lost in the pain that was now flooding his body, flowing through him like blood and running into every part of his being.

As the tendrils worked their way up his neck, crawling through arteries and into his brain, he heard the pounding of great drums and sudden shifts of colour flashed before his eyes. His hands shuddered once, then let go, and he crashed to the floor before being dragged over to the stone where the rest of the tendrils coiled about him like a snared fly in a spiderweb.

McKenzie was aware of none of that. His mind was lost in a void – a vision of an expanse of black, deep and unending, punctuated only by pinpricks of light. As the cosmos opened up before him he felt the pulse and throb of his heart like never before, smelt the taint of blood in the air, all to the unaccountable pounding of drums. It was as though he were now moving through that unending void, past countless long dead worlds and past indistinct shapes that moved and swam and churned in the abyssal darkness between the stars and galaxies. As the stench of blood grew stronger – so strong he tasted it now – he felt his body shrinking, diminishing within that endless night, surrounded by stars so old none had witnessed their birth. He tried to scream, but no sound escaped his lungs, and only that mocking drumming answered his silent cry as he faded into microscopic insignificance before the absolute vastness of time and space. A final scream welled up within him, a sense of great pressure building with it – like he might burst at any second. He was now so small he was less than an atom, moving unseen through a cosmos so immense and alien he couldn't even begin to comprehend it. He understood then the transient and futile nature of human endeavour, as they swarmed and struggled like insects to make a dent, a mark, on a universe so old and vast as to be untouchable, unknowable and uncaring. The span of human history amounted to nothing compared to such an unending ageless expanse, and the stark realisation of the futility of all that had ever been achieved threatened to overwhelm him. He tried again to move, to make any kind of sound – but he was powerless to effect any change, spiralling down into the dark void of the abyss with the tattered edges of his sanity shredding away as he went. Desperately he tried to hold onto his mind and his thoughts, but there was so little left of him now. He was shrinking away so fast, his very consciousness unravelling even as his body broke apart…

…and then he was gone.

Back in the lab McKenzie's body was moving – shambling forward, guided by the tendrils that now emerged from the back of its head as it wrenched open cabinets and drawers, collecting scalpels, spatulas, fuses and any tools and equipment that it could lay its hands on. Already the flesh was beginning to char, the body corrupting and breaking down as a result of the energy being channelled through it.

"N'gal thul'sath Nyarrrhtep d'thuu!" it cried, forcing an alien tongue through human vocal chords as best it could as it assembled the gathered items, working as swiftly as it was able to. It discarded all but three of the items it had gathered, and carried these back over to the stone – crouching awkwardly on unfamiliar bipedal limbs to begin adjusting those nubs of crystal with the crude tools it had retrieved.

The electrical fire in the corner spread rapidly now – covering the whole wall and the ceiling with searing flames, greedily consuming the piles of notes, wall-charts and furniture and spilling out into the lab next door. With nobody around to stop it, and with the doors not properly closed, there was nothing to halt its destructive progress.

McKenzie's whole body was withering away, the flesh sinking even as it blackened and peeled from the bone. Still it worked on, adjusting those exposed sections of crystal – and now a strange high pitched frequency sang out from within the heart of that device, and new sections of the pillar opened up as rods of a clear crystalline structure emerged, glowing faintly as energy coursed through them.

The collapsing form that once had been McKenzie's body shuffled around to the side of the unit. The edges of its lab coat caught alight, but still it pressed on despite the flames now running up its back, desperately trying to access some fresh nodules of crystal that were now emerging from the rear of the pillar.

It slumped awkwardly onto the floor, the head and arms burning, still struggling to twist the ends of the nodules with a scavenged pair of pliers.

A faint low rumble arose from the centre of the stone, and that fleshy heart started to pound furiously as black veins pulsed across the surface of the pillar.

A few feet in front of the device a light flared, as though being projected by those glowing crystalline rods, and the air around it rippled as if from a heat distortion.

"N'gal… th…" McKenzie's cracking throat whispered and then the blazing corpse toppled backwards, flames consuming it entirely as the pliers and equipment clattered and rolled across the floor.

The projected light swiftly widened until it formed a screen of sickly-yellow radiance in the centre of the room, less than an inch off the floor. It spread outwards, flowing over the lab benches, flaring and shifting through the visible and invisible light spectrums as it opened up, six feet across and seven feet high. From out of that strange portal a faint buzzing timbre filled the air, growing steadily in magnitude as the forming aperture took shape. With each pulse and ripple a little of the acrid smoke from within the room was sucked into the light, and a dark black fog that sank immediately down to the floor spilled out in return.

Then something else emerged, like some obscene newborn slithering from a hellish womb – a tarry viscous mass that bubbled and seethed, oozed out with the fog, running across the floor like a mucous-coated oil-slick whose surface glistened with an iridescent sheen. It slid soundlessly across the floor, stirring up the fog, heading straight for the pillar of stone. It reached the side of the device and slid up it, forming long tube-like appendages which it now slotted into the grooves on the pillar.

In the heart of the lab the aperture of pale light shimmered once again as a gnarled crab-like appendage protruded into the room amidst another burst of heavy black fog, the reddish carapace gleaming in the firelight as the rest of it emerged – a mass of feelers, a seething cluster of segmented legs….

In the adjoining lab, the flames finally reached the stored oxygen and gas cylinders and licked hungrily at their sides even as the burning ceiling collapsed in around them.

The explosion, when it came, tore through almost half the facility, blasting the windows clean out across the parking lot, and caused the upper floors to give way in a thunderous cloud of smoke, debris and flame that shook the earth and could be seen and heard for miles, and which even woke the rest of the McKenzie family from their sleep.

*

In the days that followed, the nearby town of Eastridge got very little rest – from the job losses at the destroyed facility, to the government investigation that swooped down onto the town almost as soon as the flames were out, the safe and normal routines of daily life had been shattered for the majority of the inhabitants. For days the whole town felt numb and shocked, unwelcoming of the probing and the questions by officials and wanting only to get shattered lives back on track. Most were at least grateful that the explosion had occurred so late at night – only two scientists and a security guard had been killed. But that was small comfort to their families, who looked up at that charred ruin up on the hill through grief-stricken eyes before heading home to lay one less place at the table.

But for many the losses were light, and most were thankful it hadn't been even more serious.

Thankful that is, until the first of the pets, and then shortly after children, started to go missing from back yards.

And soon after that, from within locked homes.

Regressives

We crouched atop the cliffs overlooking the landing port, our faces streaked with dirt and sweat, our crumpled clothes torn and muddied, breathing in the fume-filled air and watching the blazing lights of the cargo ships and shuttles as they cut through the stillness of the night with a roar and a rush of air and heat. We couldn't stay long, even though we loved watching the lights dancing through the darkness of the night. Sooner or later we would be detected, and hunters would be sent to apprehend us.

"Let's get back to the forest," Jerran said, picking at the damp tangles in my hair, and I laughed, loving his closeness as he loved mine.

"Already?" I answered playfully. "Thought I'd worn you out."

He grinned, putting a hand on my leg, and I felt a stirring down below in response.

"Seems neither of us is worn out yet," he teased, noting my renewed interest.

We had just had sex, out in a clearing in the deep mossy forest, almost tearing each other's clothes off in our desperate and primal need for each other. We could never have been together like this had we remained in the colony. Same-sex relationships were taboo under Genomic law. It was only here – out amidst the trees and under the stars with the night air caressing our skin - that we had finally found the freedom to be who we truly were, and to love and live as our hearts desired.

When he laughed again, I saw his canines had finally started to lengthen, like my own, and I shivered in delight. He had truly embraced his animal nature. He really was becoming one of us.

"We should go to the lagoon," he suggested. "The others will be there."

"Let's stay a little longer."

"We've been here too long already."

There was caution in his voice, and knew he was right, but I was reckless and defiant. Why should we have to live in fear just for being different? We had done nothing wrong, and yet they hounded us at every turn because we had chosen to abandon what they deemed civilised and divinely sanctioned. We had rejected their rule of law and their imposed way of life, and for that we were heretics, our rights forfeit. But even more than all of that, in their eyes we were no longer truly human, and that made us a threat to all they believed in.

It had all started with the Brethabi. Our ancestors had travelled to this world three centuries ago, escaping from the dying Earth and forging a new colony under the watchful guidance of the Genomic Church. Some of those early settlers had befriended the native species, a race called the Brethabi. Although none of us alive now had ever seen one, we had all heard the stories of their enchanting and exotic beauty. A beauty which had proved too alluring for many of the first settlers, and even knowing the risks of defying the law they had taken the associations deeper still. Unsurprisingly, such developments had outraged the Genomicists, who viewed any pollution of the human genome as a blasphemy. Almost immediately new laws had been enforced, and when that failed to stop the problem violence came swiftly after it. Of course, the Genomicists denied all responsibility for the terrible atrocities that followed: the slaughter and destruction of the native towns, and the massacre of hundreds of Brethabi, but everyone knew it had been them, fuelled by the fear that the sacred genetic code of so-called 'pure' humanity, that ultimate divine gift, might be corrupted by such liaisons. But it was too late. The bridge had been crossed and, against all the odds, those illicit liaisons with an alien race actually produced viable offspring. To compound that 'crime', many who bore such children failed to report them as they had been ordered, and so strains of alien DNA became introduced into the population, where they proved surprisingly difficult to detect and trace.

Those of us who had the Brethabi taint were often able to conceal it well into adulthood. Within most it lay dormant, but for those in which it became active, it awoke latent qualities buried deep in our genetic makeup, and fuelled a burning animal desire to escape from the confines of colony life and live free amongst the wilds of the planet as the Brethabi had.

My father had carried the dormant taint in his blood, yet it me it had become active, quickly manifesting in small but subtle ways shortly after my ninth birthday. I had been able to hide it for years, but the active taint was a progressive condition. I quickly found my sense of smell and hearing sharpening beyond human norms, my canines elongated and my vision improved too – especially at night. I craved the fresh air and the outside world more and more, finding the enclosed apartments too confining, the processed air too sterile, and would take long walks in the forest at night, sneaking out past the guards that watched the perimeter of the colony. Finally I could deny the changes no longer, and knowing it would only be a matter of time before I was discovered I had fled the colony - and Jerran, unwilling to be left behind, and blessed with the taint himself, had followed me every step of the way. I was so glad he had. He was the one reason I had endured life in the colony for so long.

"Come on, Cyrus!" Jerran prompted again, as an old passenger shuttle soared overhead, "It's not worth the risk."

Grudgingly I relented, disappointed that I had not caught any sounds or scents of my father, who worked for the docking control here. I had not seen him or my mother since fleeing the colony seven months ago, and I missed them both. We were just turning to head back into the cover of the tree line when we both froze, catching an unfamiliar scent on the night air.

I cocked my head, listening to the night around us, holding my breath.

Close by a twig snapped, the sound sudden and sharp as a gunshot to our sensitive ears, and Jerran shot me an alarmed glance.

They had found us.

We turned and fled, hearts pounding and adrenaline surging as we dashed through the trees, darting between hanging sheets of dense brackle-moss and ducking under the thick coiling roots of the marsh trees. Ahead of us, a pack of spiny-legged grevis scurried away into the night, disappearing into their burrows with a shill, alarmed shrieking - a sound that matched the keening sense of terror screaming out from deep within me. Thorny branches slashed at our skin and faces - but we didn't dare slow down, we couldn't risk even a moment's hesitation.

Behind us we heard the sounds of people giving chase, the clunk of military boots thudding on fallen tree trunks and scrunching through the thick leaf-litter, the hiss and crackle of radio chatter. Flashlight beams lanced through the darkness. Then, barely audible even to us, was the faint but steady whirring we had both been dreading – search drones, tiny automated cameras equipped with darts that the Genomicists often employed in their searches of the forest. While our enhanced senses could usually detect the clumsy approach of humans before they got close enough to strike, the drones were fast and harder to detect, harder to hear as well, if you weren't actively listening for them.

Jerran looked at me, eyes wide with terror.

"The swamp!" I hissed. It was the only thing I could think of. The drones locked in on body heat, and I hoped that the cold water of the swamp might lower our body temperatures enough to throw them off.

We sped silently through the darkness, weaving and slipping between the trees, our hearts racing and our ears ringing with the rush of blood surging through our veins. It was exhilarating, but also terrifying – we knew if we were caught our lives were as good as over. We bounded up a small craggy incline, feet moving lithely over the mossy rocks, before plunging waist-deep into the murky swamp on the other side. It was so cold that for a moment it robbed me of breath, numbing my legs almost instantly. But we struggled on – finally throwing ourselves fully into the gritty water regardless of the cold and swimming as quickly as we could.

It was then that I heard the sound overhead as a drone passed by. I almost missed it, but Jerran's ears were sharp and he grabbed my arm, dragging me under the surface. We held our breath, grabbing handfuls of weed to keep ourselves anchored below the water, and we waited. In the gritty murk we were blind and deaf to the world above. The cold pressed in all around us. The occasional unseen thing brushed past our legs and the burning need to breathe tormented our lungs.

We stayed under the water until we could endure it no longer, finally bursting up for air. We surfaced blindly, not knowing what might be waiting for us. We could only hope we had stayed under long enough and that the drone and the hunters had moved away. Blinking and gasping, I surveyed the area around us, casting glances at all the shadows, of which there were far too many. But the air was clear of any human scent, and though we strained our ears, we picked up no sound of any more drones.

"Have they gone?" Jerran whispered.

"I think so."

We hauled ourselves out of the freezing water and crouched behind a tree, shivering and soaked, listening to the night around us. Our hearts still pounding and our frozen bodies shaking and painfully numb, and we clung to each other for reassurance as much as warmth. Neither of us could relax, and not just because we were freezing. We knew the Genomicists rarely gave up the chase once they had found any Regressives. They would still be out here, combing the forest until daybreak at least – and maybe beyond that.

We both knew better than to try and make for the warm geothermal lagoons now, though we both very much wanted to be warm again and in the company of friends. We couldn't risk leading the Genomicists there. It was where most of our 'tribe' were presently based, though we knew of at least two other small tribes of Regressives that were camping out in the rocky canyons further north, and with whom we traded smuggled supplies occasionally.

"We should head south, to the caves," Jerran suggested softly, and I nodded. It was the best place to seek shelter. There were dozens of hiding spaces with plenty of dry moss and flint for starting a fire, and we knew them like the backs of our hands. The only drawback was they were quite a walk from here, and we had no idea which way the hunters and the drones had gone.

We walked in silence for what felt like hours, keeping close to the trees and rocks where possible, moving with a slow caution that was an agony in itself, wanting only to slip into the protective shelter of the caves where we could relax and breathe freely again.

We were almost at the caves, our goal virtually in sight, when I saw it - a tiny red speck flickering on the back of Jerran's neck.

I went to push him aside, the warning cry already forming in my throat, when something stung the back of my own neck with a sharp scratch. My hand flew up to the small metal dart that was now jutting from my skin even as my legs wobbled and buckled under me. In my rapidly blurring vision, Jerran stumbled too, and twisting my head against the growing numbness I caught a glimpse of someone up in the branches above us, downwind of our position, dressed in dark clothing and lowering a rifle.

Then everything went black.

We awoke in a strange room. Cold and stark, all metal and concrete, smelling of disinfectant and chemicals. The lights above us were too bright, and sounds echoed off the walls. As our vision steadied and our memories emerged slowly from the haze, we saw we were surrounded by six armed Genomicists - we recognised their uniforms at once - and a sudden panic flooded through me.

They forced us to strip, without dignity or compassion, taking away our old familiar clothes to be burned, before hosing us down with a stinging jet of icy water. They then tossed us some baggy, strange-smelling and uncomfortable orange coveralls to wear. Quietly we slipped into them, too scared, shaking and humiliated to say anything, and they clamped restraint bracelets on our wrists before herding us roughly over to two waiting cells.

I knew then, as I watched them draw the metal gate shut on my cell and felt the restraint bracelets tighten painfully, that the best we could hope for now was sterilisation and testing - their constant search to find a way to undo the dormant 'contamination' that lurked amongst their pure human colonists. I just hoped that the terrible rumours we had all heard about the massive incinerators deep beneath the complex were just that, but as I looked at Jerran's pale face in the next cell I could see the same fears reflected there. I tried to reach my fingers through to touch his, to offer what little reassurance I could, but the gaps between the metal mesh were too small and the restraint bracelets restricted my movement.

"I'm sorry," I whispered, knowing how hollow those words sounded after the situation I had got us both into.

"Don't be," he said, offering a faint smile. "I'm glad for what we had, no matter what happens now. I don't regret it."

My heart broke then, and I wished I could have held him close. How like Jerran not to hold any resentment or blame. He didn't have a hateful cell in his body. But still I felt guilty for dragging him into all this. If only I had listened to him back at the spaceport. He might not blame me for that, but I did.

"I won't let them hurt you," I vowed. "I'll get you out of this."

I just wished I knew how. There had been several attempts in the past to break Regressives out of Genomicist holding cells, but none had ever been successful. Even those people in the colonies who were secretly sympathetic to us and who smuggled us clothing and medical supplies from time to time, had been unable to help us get past the high security of the Genomic facilities. The Genomicists controlled the technology and were the only ones allowed to bear arms. Against them, we didn't stand a chance.

"How long do you think it's been since they brought us in?" he said miserably, staring up at the ceiling. "Think it's still night out there?"

"Try not to think about that," I urged gently, but the truth was I was trying not to think about it myself. I would have given anything for a window right then, just a glimpse of the sky and the trees in place of those glaring lights and that cold ceiling.

"What are we going to do?"

I didn't answer. I knew he was seeking reassurances, and I had none. In truth, I didn't blame him for seeking some glimmer of hope to cling onto. I needed one myself. In my heart I knew we would never again see the sky or feel the fresh breeze on our faces as we ran through the forests. The freedom we loved was gone now, as was all hope of a future, replaced with concrete walls and steel bars in a room that smelled strongly of detergent, piss and fear, a lasting legacy of the innocent lives that had suffered and ended here. It was a fortress of hate and intolerance, and it was all around us, as though it had soaked into the metal and stone of the very foundations of the place.

For hours we sat in terrified silence, huddled up against the bars, as close to each other as we could be, wondering what was going to happen. There was no way to mark the passage of time or to know for sure how long we had been there – the room always looked the same and the lights never changed, but our stomachs were growling and our throats were parched and dry in the processed air.

Then with a *whoosh* that made us both jump the large metal doors at the end of the room parted and a small group of Genomicists marched inside. They opened Jerran's cage and stabbed a tranquiliser pen into his arm. They dragged him, kicking and thrashing, out of the cage before it even took effect. I protested, pleading and shaking at the cage doors until my throat hurt and my voice was hoarse – but they ignored me, hauling Jerran away even as he howled in terror. By now his body was going limp, and I screamed with my failing voice for them not to hurt him, but they dragged him across the floor like he was just a sack of refuse and then they were gone.

I don't know how long I sat staring at those doors after that. I was shaking with rage and with fear, but powerless to fight back. Worst of all, I didn't know if I would see Jerran again, or what they were doing to him. I could only hope they weren't hurting him. I no longer cared about myself – but Jerran, this was my fault, and I knew that whatever came I had to try and get him out of this, somehow, if it wasn't already too late. I couldn't stand the thought that he might be suffering because of my stupidity. The guilt was haunting me like a ghost, whispering as though it were a physical presence there in that confined space with me.

For a long time I just lay there, curled on the floor, watching the door without moving. My hunger had now become a constant hollow ache and a throbbing headache pulsed behind my eyes. My bladder was also giving me signs that it would like to be emptied, but there was nowhere to go, so I held on. I didn't want to give the Genomicists the satisfaction of seeing me soil myself like some frightened caged beast. Despite the exhaustion that threatened to claim me, I couldn't sleep. Fear and guilt gnawed at me, and behind them was an overwhelming sense of panic that I was somehow barely managing to hold at bay.

Then, just as I was pacing to take my mind off of the hunger and the growing need to urinate, I heard a faint noise from a far corner of the room and saw someone – a woman - slipping quietly towards my cage. Immediately I took a step back, recognising the uniform of a Genomicist scientist, but then I stopped, sniffing the air in surprise. My visitor was not entirely human. I smelled the Brethabi taint about her. The taint was subtle in its outward manifestations, in most it resulted only in a more acute sense of taste, hearing and smell, the lengthening of the canines, an increased agility and a thickening of body hair – but it also affected the body's pheromones, and those with the taint could always tell another of their kind.

"Don't be scared," she said, glancing around as she reached the front of my cage. "I won't hurt you."

"Who are you?"

"I'm going to let you out, but you have to come with me."

"No," I said, more sharply than I intended. "I can't. They took my friend."

"I know."

"I won't leave without him."

"I'll take you to him, but you must follow me."

"But what-?" I began, but she shook her head.

"No time to talk, we must hurry."

She drew a security card from her pocket and ran it over the door sensor. I watched in silence as the bars slid open, my heart hammering and confusion, hope and fear surging chaotically within me. I wanted so badly to believe this was freedom, but how could I trust it?

"Well, come on," she urged.

She unlocked my restraints and then we moved like shadows across the room. For the first time since my arrival I finally saw the full size of it. The sight of the rows of cages stretching down the length of the place filled me with a cold dread. They were all empty now, but the implication of so many of them was horrifying. I wondered if they had ever once been full – or, more alarmingly, were they in preparation for things to come?

"You're a Genomicist?" I whispered as we ducked into a small dimly-lit access hallway.

"I am," she nodded.

"But you're not pure human."

"They don't know about my condition. I've been able to hide it, for now – I had my canines removed and false ones implanted, and the other signs, you can hide them if you're careful."

"You say that like it's a disease."

"In my position it may as well be."

"It's nothing to be ashamed of."

"It's nothing I chose to be, either," she said frostily, and I quickly let the matter drop.

She guided me down to a small intersection of hallways and gestured off to the right.

"Your friend is down there. Third door on the left."

"Is it safe?" I asked warily. The whole place reeked of the pungent stench of disinfectant and was preventing me from getting a good sense of whether we were alone down here.

She nodded softly. "It's late. Everybody's gone home apart from a handful of night-shift workers."

Warily, I opened the door and peered inside, gazing out upon two rows of gleaming silver surgical beds surrounded by banks of darkened machinery, all except for one bed at the far end of the room upon which a single form lay, covered up to the neck by a thin sheet. Unconsciously I sniffed the air, checking for danger and searching for Jerran's scent.

"There's nobody else here," she said softly, and as though that had been the sign I had been waiting for I raced along the avenue of empty beds to the motionless form in the furthest one.

It was Jerran. I almost didn't recognise him with his head shaved and a mass of wires and electrodes connected to it, but I was close enough now to clearly distinguish his scent over the chemicals that the room reeked of. It was then that I spotted the two machines on the left side of the bed. One was drawing out his blood and pumping it away into some kind of an analyser, but the other machine was replacing it with some kind of pale, synthetic plasma.

"Jerran," I said, gently touching the side of his face, "It's me."

He turned his face slowly and looked at me blankly.

"It's Cyrus," I whispered, but again there was nothing. No recognition, no hint of awareness. It felt then like someone had slugged me in the gut and driven all the air from my lungs. My legs were suddenly weak and shaky, as if I would topple at any second.

"What have they done to him?" I asked, glancing angrily at the woman who now stood beside me.

"I'm sorry, there's nothing we can do now."

I blinked, struggling to comprehend her meaning. "What?"

"It's too late."

"No," I shook my head furiously. "No – you've got to help him. Get these things out of him, and stop whatever they are doing…"

"No, you don't understand. The chemicals they are flushing into him are a poison - painless, but deadly. I can't stop what's been started."

"But, he's…. no."

"He's already gone. His body just doesn't know it yet. And his blood is being pumped away for analysis."

I tried to speak, but couldn't. Tried to swallow, but I couldn't do that either. The rage that had been building like a growing wall of pressure within me suddenly collapsed upon itself, leaving a hollow emptiness in its wake.

"No," I managed at last, not quite a whisper, but not much more. I stared down into the face of the man I loved and something died inside. He was watching me now, blinking occasionally, but again there was no awareness in his eyes, no sense that he was really seeing or hearing any of what was going on. I sank to the floor at the side of the bed. I had nothing left. No fight, no energy, no desire to even stand up again. What was left for me without him? I took his hand in mine, and was still holding it when his breathing stopped a few minutes later.

For a while the woman left me there, still holding his hand, and I in all honesty had completely forgotten she was even there. But then finally I felt her fingers rest gently on my shoulder.

"Can you stand?"

I shook my head.

"You need to try. We don't have long, it'll be dawn soon."

I wondered why I should care.

"I couldn't help him," she said softly, "but I can help you."

"There's nothing left for me," I whispered.

"I meant all of you, everyone still out there."

I looked up. She was holding a needle in one hand and a thin glass vial in the other, and while I couldn't see what was written on the vial, the needle smelled of sedative.

"I can make us whole again – human once more. Help us find our path back to the light."

"You – you did this?" I blinked in disbelief, my dazed senses finally waking from the shock and grief that had swallowed them.

"I didn't kill him," she protested, watching my reaction carefully. "I was trying to cure him. When it failed, the others decided his suffering had to be ended. But I know I can find a cure, that's why I came for you. They were going to euthanize you in the morning too. They've decided my project is not worth pursuing, that there is no way to reverse the active taint. Let me show them that there is a chance for those of you who are lost out there. You can be saved."

"Stay away from me!" I warned, rising shakily to my feet.

"The Genomicists aren't your enemies. We only want to bring you back on the path of purity."

"How can you do this to your own kind?"

"We're not a kind of anything, don't you see? We have no rights and no place, in this or any world. We are a mistake, an abomination. A corruption of a divine form. Something diseased that needs to be cured and healed."

"What we were," I said, struggling to find the words, fighting the boiling rage that had returned and burned upwards through my body, "was *happy*. We were happy – do you understand that? We wanted to be left alone, that's all. We're not a threat to you, or a mistake. But you – none of you – can leave us alone, can you? You'll never stop hounding us while we still draw breath."

"We can't do that," she shook her head. "It wouldn't be right. The sanctity of the human genetic code cannot be disputed. It is our duty to protect it, and to help cleanse those who have become tainted as we have!"

A white hot rush of rage seared through me, and clenched my hands until my nails bit deep into my flesh, letting the pain fuel my anger and grief.

"Let me help you," she urged again, moving toward me, the needle glinting brightly.

"Stay the hell away from me!"

"I can give you back the life that was denied you."

Anxiously I glanced around, desperately seeking something to defend myself with. I knew she would have the agility and speed of a Regressive, this wouldn't be like trying to evade a human. It was then that I saw the movement from the corner of my eye – as soon as my gaze had been directed elsewhere she had lunged for me, preparing to jab the sedative into my arm. Instinctively I sprang sideways, and the tip of the needle narrowly missed me. It was then I saw the metal tray, loaded with vials of various kinds, and I snatched it up, scattering the glass tubes across the floor and shattering them. I swung the metal tray around as hard and fast as I could, and it connected with the side of her skull. She went sprawling, crashing onto the bed that still held Jerran's lifeless form – the needle skittering away across the lab floor – and as she staggered to her feet the sheet covering his naked body slipped away. Deep incisions riddled his flesh where tissue had been removed for testing.

"It's not what it looks like," she said quickly. "I tried to protest – but we needed the data. We need to understand the progression of the genetic …"

I never gave her the chance to finish. I charged at her, a frenzied roar of grief and maddened fury exploding from my throat, and I slammed the now twisted tray down across her head as hard as I could manage. She crumpled like a puppet whose strings had been cut, and I let the tray drop to the floor beside her, tears streaming down my face and my whole body shaking and trembling.

I don't know how long I stood there. Time had no meaning any more, and my whole body was shocked and numb. Finally something of my senses reawakened and I looked down as though seeing her for the first time. I checked her wrist and found a pulse, strong and steady, and knew she was just unconscious. For a second I thought about wiring her up to one of those machines and giving her the same fate she and her colleagues had given to Jerran, but instead I left her on the floor and took only her security card. I wanted to take Jerran too, but I knew I would have a hard enough time getting myself out, let alone trying to sneak his body out with me. In the end I took a handful of his shorn hair from a container next to the bed and then left quietly.

She had been right about the building being on a skeleton crew for the night shift. With my enhanced hearing and sight it was relatively easy to slip past the lumbering human patrols, especially as their guard was down, and all of the automated cameras made a distinctive whirring sound that my enhanced hearing detected long before I even came close to them. My one fear was that they might employ the same heat-sensing technology that the drones did. The shadows would not conceal me against that. But fortunately it seemed the Genomicists had put most of their security measures into keeping people out of the building, and hadn't in their arrogance considered anybody would try to escape from within. In the end I managed to subdue a patrolling guard, and once I had relieved him of his slightly too-large uniform and security card, I found and opened a locked skylight. It was then that I made my near-fatal mistake. At the sight of those trees and the smell of the fresh air outside, I lunged forward for that opening – spotting too late the fine mesh of lasers that blocked my escape. As it sliced three fingers clean off of my left hand a white-hot pain lanced through me and I dropped back down, howling with agonised surprise. For a few seconds I crouched there, whimpering and holding my hand close to my chest, tears stinging my eyes and my body shaking. With my heart hammering in my chest I examined my left hand fearfully. The wound had been immediately cauterised, but my only my thumb and forefinger remained intact, the rest were little more than oddly-angled stumps. I stared at my hand for what felt like an eternity, not quite believing what I was seeing. The remains of my fingers lay scattered on the floor, and for one insane second I almost went to gather them up – but then came the hastily approaching footsteps. I knew guards had been alerted by my cries. It was then that I spotted the deactivation switch and frantically swiped my stolen card over it. I pounced for the opening, kicking and struggling as I hauled myself through, finally managing to get up into the trees beside the structure. It was an escape only a Regressive could have achieved, and now that it had happened once, I knew the Genomicists would never allow it to happen again.

*

My father had always taught me to stand up for what I believed to be right, and to use anger as a means to open people's eyes instead of causing violence and misery. I wanted to stay true to his wisdom. To use the anger and outrage to fuel a wiser response, to turn this crime into a positive fight and not give in to hatred and vengeance. But my wounds were too deep and too fresh for me to think that way yet. I was hurt and I wanted to hurt them back. To wound them as deeply as they had wounded me. Until the grief and pain had subsided, I knew rational and reasonable thought were not going to find ground to grow.

I stood slowly, rising from beside the simple earthen mound that was now the only physical reminder I had of the man I loved. It seemed such an inadequate marker for all that he had been, all that he might have been, and all that he had meant to me – but it was all I had; just a tiny mound of earth over a few cuttings of hair.

I glanced down at my ruined hand, balling it into as much of a fist as I could manage. It hurt, and I was glad. The pain and anger were all that fuelled me right now.

Then I left that place, heading deeper into the forest. I didn't look back. I couldn't have faced the prospect of going on without Jerran, never seeing or speaking to him again, if I had time to reflect upon it. So I kept moving, forcing myself to focus on only one thought: The surviving Brethabi tribes were still out there, somewhere, though they had been driven far from our colonies, and I would find them and ask for their aid. Whatever it took, and no matter how far I had to go. I would seek them out and ask them to unite with us against our common enemy.

We were kin after all.

Automated Relay

Eric Graven frowned, scratching at the dark stubble on his chin as he peered at the tiny green display screen, watching lines of digits blink before his eyes as they fed back a system status report.

That can't be right.

He patted the pockets of his grey technician's jacket absent-mindedly as he hunted for a cigarette, finally finding what he was looking for in the leg-pockets of his grubby khaki trousers. The lighter sparked into life, a brief flare of light and warmth in an otherwise cold and dimly lit space.

Officially he wasn't allowed to smoke inside the station's mainframe, but since they wouldn't find out about it he figured there was no harm.

He hated the old X-14 automated orbital relay stations with a passion, and vowed silently never to get called out to another. He much preferred the large manned stations – with their heaters, vending machines, vidnets and other comforts. He was lucky if these remote automated places even had a head fitted. Even the minimal life support systems they boasted were cut back to the absolute minimum to save on power consumption, and then only activated once maintenance personnel were about to go aboard. Sure, the old X-14s were marvels of cost-effective efficiency, but nobody ever seemed to care about the basic needs of the technicians who would have to spend hours in them whenever they needed maintenance.

"This shit's no way to make a living," he muttered to the systems regulator console as he eased himself behind it. The space was tight, claustrophobic and thoroughly uninviting, but at least it didn't look like he was going to need the cutter from his toolbox on this job. The panels, bolts and bulkheads all opened easily enough and there were no signs of any obvious internal damage to any of the hardware.

In all of his thirty-five years, the last sixteen had been spent clambering around behind dusty machinery and circuits or crawling deep into the bowels of access conduits trying to trace elusive faults and malfunctions. At first it had all sounded too good to be true – travelling with the science vessels and cargo haulers out to distant worlds and remote outposts, mining stations and research bases. The lure of journeying among the stars seeing the alien and exotic wonders of the galaxy first-hand, instead of staying on a colony world and eking a living as a farmer or mechanic, had been too strong to resist. But the reality that had all too quickly become apparent was that his 'stunning' view of the wonders of the universe usually amounted to little more than a dingy computer room, a cramped mainframe conduit or the rear of a malfunctioning device in some windowless sub-level closet.

Ghk'k'rrrrr...

The noise cut through the room, a cross between the hiss and crackle of static and someone trying to speak whilst choking.

What the hell? He glared over at the transmission display. It was hard to tell from his position but it looked normal, and wasn't showing any incoming or outgoing signals. *Hell, don't tell me the transmitter's picked up a glitch as well.*

He tugged his right glove off with his teeth while he unhooked the battered communications unit from his belt, before keying in his user ID. "This is Graven, still no luck finding the source of that damn power fluctuation. Also, think the transmitter might be screwing around as well. Gonna be a few more hours at least."

"This is Administrator Malcolms," the tinny voice crackled back. Even with the poor reception, it oozed officiousness. "Keep us apprised. We'll swing back by the system in four hours for an update. Let us know if you need any extra assistance over there."

Bite me, you smug jackass, Eric scowled at the unit.

"Graven? You copy?" Malcolms prompted.

"Yeah. Will do," he said sharply as he cut off the transmission.

He knew Henry Malcolms far better than he wanted to – an officious pen pusher with a squishy toad-like face and a constant smirk who kept warm behind his desk while sending others out to do the real work, for which he often took credit.

Eric left the communications unit sitting on top of one of the consoles as he set about checking the integrity of the power distribution conduits. It was tedious work. He shivered as he ran the traces, wishing the technicians' uniforms were thicker, even the jackets they provided did little to keep out the chill. The cold of space seeped into everything out here, and was an unwelcome reminder of just how thin and vulnerable the walls were that separated him from the lifeless icy vacuum outside. The minutest breech or malfunction in the hull of the station or with any of the seals, the tiniest strike from a fragment of meteor, and life would be over pretty fast.

He shuffled uncomfortably from foot to foot as he worked, stopping every few moments to rub his hands together. Even with the gloves on the chill found a way to bite into his flesh and numb his body. Then he frowned – there was no putting it off any longer.

Unzipping his fly, he urinated around the back of the primary buffer, breathing a long sigh of relief. He was fairly sure it wouldn't affect any of the equipment, and the evidence would be long gone by the time the next engineer came in here.

Teach 'em not to install a damn head, he smiled, watching the rising steam.

That was when he heard the beeping of an alarm from the other side of the unit, interspersed by a crackling and popping hiss of static.

Ghk'k'rrrrr… Ghk'k'rrrrr…

He jumped, nearly dousing his boots, and glanced over at the display readout. His confusion doubled; several of the systems that he had personally shut down during his earlier diagnostic checks were now powered up and running again.

What the-?

He zipped himself up and hurried to the readout screen, his boots clanging hollowly on the deck plates. He checked each of the display consoles with growing irritation. According to the instruments, the system was processing an incoming signal – but he knew all such functions had been deactivated for the duration of his maintenance work.

"I'm not in the mood for this!" he snapped at the console, treating it to one of his sternest scowls and giving it a hefty thump with his gloved hand.

Ghk'k'rrrrr… Gh'rrr… Ghrar…

The screen flickered, the internal speakers sputtering and hissing. Around him dead instruments were bursting to life – a buzzing whine of activity as console after console whirred and surged into a frenzy of activity. The incoming signal display alone remained dead and dark, but the processing buffer and outgoing broadcast units were oscillating frantically as they processed a transmission which, according to the data supplied by all the available instruments, they had never received in the first place.

Bewildered, Eric activated the internal speakers.

Probably just feedback, but let's see.

He settled reluctantly into the icy chair, checked the readout settings, and then played the transmission.

Ghhh'rrraa… ghrar…ghrari….aa…

A savage burst of static exploded out of the speakers, deafening in the enclosed space – but the crackling static now had a deeper quality to it, almost as though a thick guttural voice, strangely warped and drawn-out, was trying to speak under the crackling distortion, and it boomed resonantly around the chamber.

Ghhh'rrraa… ghrar… aaa …ghrarirshhh…

Gritting his teeth he hit the power switch and bathed the console in darkness. The merciful silence that followed was so stark that for a second he felt numb. He took a deep breath. "Let's try again. This time, play nice," he warned the master control unit as he reinitialized each of the systems one at a time.

With his finger hovering over the power switch and the volume control cranked as low as possible, Eric ran the stored transmission once more, gradually increasing the volume as he went. At first there was nothing but the crackle of static. But as the volume increased a whispering became discernable, and as the volume grew louder still he made out the same guttural voice in the background behind the static.

Aaa…Ghrarirshhh…aaa… eeeah Ghrarirshhh

He momentarily forgot all about the cold that still chilled his body as his fingers reached for the diagnostic controls. Clearly there was either a problem in the station's receivers that was distorting the transmission, or the transmission itself was incredibly faint. He chewed busily on his lower lip as he got to work running the signal through the system amplifiers and trying to boost it whilst filtering out the background noise.

"All right," he said half an hour later, finally noticing the cold and shifting awkwardly in his seat to wake up his chilled limbs, "Let's see what we've got."

He flipped the switch and sat back. At first there was nothing, only the occasional hissing crackle, but gradually he discerned another faint sound, buried amongst the background static, and he leaned over to check the readout.

Without warning, a sound so utterly deep and inhuman it barely qualified as a voice blasted out, sending him stumbling from the chair. He caught his foot in the process and sprawled roughly onto the deck-plates. The language, if that is what it was, was an utter nonsense of thick growling syllables and glottal stops, but something about it – the tone and quality - filled him with an unaccountable terror.

Iä! Ghrai'rirsh mest'k dhu gya'h! Iä! Ghrai'rirsh n'gai!

Each twisted syllable struck him like a physical blow and slammed into his reeling mind, affecting him in ways words – or mere sounds – never should have been able to. They coiled thickly about his head, invading his thoughts and clouding his vision. It was as though those sounds managed to pierce and invade the veils of his subconscious in some shocking and unaccountable way - filling his mind with a darkness that left his limbs shaking and his body slick with perspiration, even in the chilled atmosphere of the processor. The wild grip of madness seized him as strange thoughts and unclear images flashed darkly through his head, cutting through the civilized veneer and exposing the instinctual primal and animalistic fears that dwelled deep within. There were flashes of movement like something coiled and foully wormlike that was flexing and stirring in some deep dark space, strange visions of blazing braziers surrounded by dancing silhouettes that twisted and contorted into monstrous shapes beneath an alien sky, and he heard the crazed and frenzied wailing of tongues that could not have been human, and beyond it all a shrill and thin whining that he could not account for.

His heart was pounding so hard and fast it seemed any moment it would explode, and the room span as though he were trapped on some demented fairground ride. His fingers gripped tightly at the deck-plates and his ears rang from the assault.

Iä! Ghrai'rirsh mest'k dhu gya'h! Iä! Ghrai'rirsh n'gai! Rag'hsta'k mest'k dhu gya'h!

With a frenzied scream he clamped his hands over his ears, frantically striving to block out the sounds, but all to no avail. The sounds were *everywhere* now – not just filling his ears as they had filled the space of the room, but they were in his skin, his blood – as though they had saturated and permeated every physical thing within the station itself. They had shifted beyond being simple sound-waves and their essence was soaking into the matter of the station just as water soaks into a sponge. That guttural chant sounded with each pulse of his heart, each breath he took, and even with each blink of his eyes. His skin felt greasy with it. A foul and acrid taste clung to his tongue.

Iä! Ghrai'rirsh mest'k dhu gya'h! Iä! Ghrai'rirsh n'gai! Rag'hsta'k mest'k dhu gya'h! Iä! Ghrai'rirsh! Iä! Ghrai'rirsh! Iä! Ghrai'rirsh rhz'ka!

He howled again as he staggered to his feet, reeling almost drunkenly he lunged for the console, strands of drool hanging from his lips and a crazed fire blazing in his eyes as he jabbed at the controls in a frenzy. One of his hands seized the volume control and silence fell across the room as he muted the signal.

He sank to his knees with a half-choked gasp, leaned over and dry retched uncontrollably, wheezing and heaving until his guts and sides ached excruciatingly from the effort. Finally he slumped against one of the bulkheads, chest rising and falling heavily and his eyes staring blankly ahead. He looked like a sagging rag-doll that had been cast aside by a petulant child.

Gradually the numbness and shock lost some of their crippling hold on him. His guts still ached and his head throbbed, but his body felt his own again. Mercifully, the visions too had ceased with the ending of the transmission.

When his body finally had the strength to move again, he wiped his mouth with the back of his hand and tried to calm his shocked and shaking nerves as he hauled himself unwillingly onto his feet.

He stumbled over towards the console where he had left the communications unit, watching the transmission display warily as though expecting it to boom into life again at any second. That inhuman voice, although now silenced, still rang in his ears.

He reached for the unit – and frowned. The whole device was covered in a strange white residue. It looked almost like pale brain matter, though of a more gelatinous consistency, and it seemed threaded with thin pulsing veins. His frown deepened. The same matter had formed on a number of the consoles, and even across some of the bulkheads.

He wiped the foul slime away, but a sharp burning sensation in his fingers made him wrench his hand back with a pained yelp. The fingers of his glove were bubbling and dissolving. In a panic he tore it off, letting it drop to the floor as he inspected his hand. It looked like a chemical or acid burn.

Son of a bitch! He cursed, angrily kicking the remains of the glove across the deck plates.

An unwelcome thought struck him and he hurriedly checked the station's hull integrity and examined the consoles and bulkheads that now had the unknown substance on them. He had horrible visions of the stuff corroding through the metal and venting the atmosphere, or burning through the life support systems or central computer core – but the systems showed the station was intact and seemed unaffected by the substance.

Screw this, he decided, pulling off his other glove and using it to press the buttons on the slime-covered communications unit.

"This is Graven," he called out, speaking at the unit rather than into it. "I've got a real problem here. There's some kind of…*stuff*. It's all over the place, and it's caustic or something – burned clean through my glove."

"This is Administrator Malcolms," the smug tones were now tinged with a hint of bewilderment. "Please clarify – what's the problem?"

"There's something – a contaminant or, well, I don't know what the hell it is, but it's everywhere."

"What kind of contaminant?"

"I just told you, I don't know!" Eric retorted. "Look, get a science team over here right away. But I want out. I'm not getting paid enough to deal with this crap."

"Calm down."

"Don't tell me to calm down!" Eric barked. "You're not the one over here!"

"Listen to me carefully, If you continue to adopt this tone…"

"No, you listen," Eric struggled to keep his voice level, "there is something *really* weird going on over here. I mean that – something *seriously* wrong!"

There was silence for a moment, but when Malcolms answered his tone was as icy as the air in the relay station. "Three hours is the quickest we can get to you. Then we'll send a science team over to check out this *contaminant*, and you and I can have a little chat about your attitude."

"Gladly," Eric acknowledged with a resentful glower before ending the transmission. In the silence that followed, he suddenly felt more isolated than he ever had at any time in his life. The prospect of those three hours sounded more like an eternity.

He threw his other glove away, it too had started to corrode. He paced restlessly, avoiding the patches of fleshy residue that were scattered around the room.

No way was that transmission a human voice, he decided. *But then what the hell did that make it? Alien?* So far the probing forays of the human race into the larger universe had turned up nothing more impressive than some new species of fungi, lichen and bacterial life, certainly nothing at a level capable of vocalizing.

He checked his watch again. Only eight minutes had passed. *This is going to be a long three hours.*

He leaned against the bulkhead over by the life support system after first checking it was clear of the corrosive slime, and tried unsuccessfully to focus his mind on other things. But the transmission was still nagging at him, and he found himself continually glancing at the console with a morbid curiosity.

Finally he pushed himself away from the wall and approached the console warily. He had no intention of replaying the transmission, but he had to know where it had come from and exactly what it was. He wasn't someone who scared easily, but that sound had affected him in a way he never would have believed possible, and he had to know how.

Both the chair and the controls looked clean and so he sat down, first ensuring the speakers were muted, and activated the trace protocol, rubbing his cold hands together as he waited.

From behind him there came a faint dragging noise – like something sliding across metal – and he glanced around, hands clenching unconsciously into fists; but the room behind him appeared empty.

Your nerves are shot to hell, he told himself, *that's all.* But even so, he shifted in his seat so that he could keep an eye on the rest of the room.

He drummed his fingers impatiently as he watched the numbers cycle on the screen. It was taking longer than usual.

The dragging noise came again, louder this time, but still he could see nothing. He was just reaching for the flashlight hooked at his belt when the computer bleeped loudly, announcing the trace was complete.

"No. That can't be right," he whispered, a shiver running down his spine.

According to the trace, the signal had originated somewhere in sector G-756.

Humanity had stretched its reach deep into space as new technologies had allowed it to overcome the almost inconceivable distances between the stars, and the myriad problems of supplying ample food, fuel and air to make the journeys possible, as well as the time such trips took to make. But still there were a great many limits to how far the human reach could extend at this point, and sector G-756 was one of them, a distant cluster of stars known only from long-range observations, and far too remote for any vessels to reach.

Eric stared in disbelief at the readouts. If the computer was right, there was no way that signal could have had a human origin after all.

But how has the signal travelled this far without degrading? Surely...

Something dropped from the ceiling, landing heavily on the console. Eric recoiled, staring at the pulsing mass that now squirmed and writhed before him. It was the size of a tennis ball, composed of the same fleshy white substance that formed all around the inside of the station. Even as he watched it exuded three thin snakelike tendrils that explored the surface around it.

Eric swallowed only to find his throat utterly dry. He backed away from unknown pulsing thing that had now extended two more tendrils and was quickly slithering up the wall.

He glanced to where the residue-coated communications unit had been resting. The corrosive slime covering it had thickened and now also showed signs of movement – faint twitches rippled spasmodically across the surface. A quick inspection of the other patches on the walls and floor revealed the same was happening in all of them.

Aware he was in danger, he moved cautiously toward one of the storage lockers, eyes scanning the floor for any more of the strange life-forms. There were at least three – one over by the life support controls and another two slithering off into the darkened corners of the station. Then he reached the locker, opened it and squeezed himself quickly inside before shutting the door.

The enclosed space was maddeningly claustrophobic and the metal shelves at the rear dug into his back. He gritted his teeth, trying to calm his racing heart. His body was slick with sweat and for the first time since he had come on board he was unpleasantly hot and clammy. He just hoped he was right about those things not being able to corrode metal.

Something shuffled against the outside of the door, and his heart froze. There was a rough dragging sound, and then a soft thud as something heavy struck the outside of the locker. Eric held his breath, the urge to pee suddenly returning with a vengeance. The scraping continued, slowly and deliberately, as though whatever was out there was meticulously and methodically exploring the entire surface of the door.

It's looking for a way in, he thought. But surely that was crazy. It had no eyes or other sensory organs – or at least none that he had seen in his brief glimpses. But still, the scraping continued – moving up and over the front of the door. Then abruptly it stopped, and the only sounds that Eric could hear were those of his own nervous swallowing and his racing heart.

Iä! Ghrai'rirsh mest'k dhu gya'h! Iä! Ghrai'rirsh n'gai!

The sound was muffled through the locker, but was unmistakable. The transmission was broadcasting again. A shiver ran through Eric, and with it came a frantic realisation. The creatures had only appeared after the transmission had been played, and now it was playing again. Would more come? Or would something even worse happen?

But what was it? A call? A summons? Something that had been echoing secretly through the void of space from some uncharted system only to be picked up by a malfunctioning relay station and broadcast accidentally by a repair technician?

A thin whine of fear escaped his lips, and his hands were clenched so tightly that his nails were cutting into his palms.

You've got to stop it, he told himself, trying to hold on to the tattered edges of his rational mind. *You've got to go out there and stop it.*

But he couldn't move. His feet were rooted and his legs refused to obey his commands. He swallowed hard and tried to battle the rising panic that was overtaking him.

More will come!

And then he was moving – spurred on by a combination of fear and adrenaline. He threw the door open and peered around the room.

The creatures were getting larger. They had reached roughly the size of a small terrier and were still growing. The largest one among them showed marked differences to the others. A ridge of rough scales had spread across it, and dark veins pulsed and throbbed beneath the surface. Its tendrils had grown to at least four feet in length, and it was running them across the consoles and in the narrow gaps between the terminals. One of those tendrils was resting on the signal controls. It had knocked some of the switches, restarting the transmission.

His stomach shrank in upon itself. *Christ, how fast are they growing? At this rate…*

His thoughts were cut short as his right foot stepped in something soft. He had trodden on one of the smaller creatures. He jumped back, shaking his foot frantically in a vain effort to dislodge it, only to discover that it had coiled itself around his boot and was now stretching questing tendrils up toward his ankle. There was a cold dampness and then an agonizing burning as the creature burned through his clothing and attacked his skin. Pain seared through him, as if his limbs had been engulfed in white-hot fire or acid. An agony so intense it stripped away all conscious thought from his mind and overwhelmed his senses. He barely managed to stop himself from instinctively reaching down and trying to claw the mass off with his hands.

He lurched clumsily across the room, searching frantically for something he might use to scrape the mass away. In desperation he thought of his toolbox. It took him a second to remember where he had left it, and he took a staggering step toward it.

Suddenly his leg collapsed beneath him, sending him crashing to the deck plates. He landed heavily, cracking his elbow and chin against the metal. He gritted his teeth to fight back the scream that was forming there, the tendons in his neck standing out like steel cables.

As he glanced down at his leg a nauseated burst of horror surged through him. He no longer had a foot. The mass had dissolved it all – bone, flesh, cloth and even his sturdy work boot, leaving only a white nub of disintegrating bone surrounded by bubbling, dripping flesh and the ragged shreds of dissolving cloth. He noticed crazily that the steel cap of his boots and the little metal loops that once held his laces had been left behind intact on the deck-plates, obviously indigestible by the mass. And now, that same dreadful amorphous mass was crawling higher.

With a frenzied, hysterical wail he flailed wildly, trying in vain to shake the substance off of his body, kicking out with his remaining leg, and slamming his body violently from left to right in a crazed frenzy of panic.

It had no effect on the gelatinous horror that was attacking him. The mass only oozed further up his leg, tightly wrapping around the limb and extending extra tendrils as it greedily searched for more matter upon which to feed.

With his eyes clouding with tears he dragged himself over to his toolbox. He scrabbled at the latch on the chest with shaking hands, and snatched up the heavy-duty cutter inside.

He activated it and angled the spinning blade down, aiming at a spot just below his knee. Sweat poured down his face as he fought to keep his shaking hands still. His breathing was harsh and ragged. He bit down on his lip and tried to brace himself as best as possible.

He made the attempt twice before he finally worked up the courage to do it, each time he had pulled the blade away at the last moment with a frightened whimpering wail.

You're gonna bleed to death! His mind shrieked at him. *If that alien thing doesn't kill you, shock and blood loss will!*

With a raw howl he shut his eyes and drove the blade into his leg, screaming as it tore through flesh and sinew. The pain was unimaginable, a searing white-hot fire that consumed all thoughts and enveloped his whole body in its agonizing embrace. The blade squealed as it hit bone, and he bit down harder, barely feeling it as his teeth punctured his lower lip. His whole body shook as white spots of light erupted behind his closed eyelids.

Ohgodohgodohgodohgod….

The air was thick with the coppery tint of blood, so thick he tasted it, but still he forced his hands – hands that now were as numb and as heavy as blocks of wood – to keep cutting downwards. His good leg was firmly braced against the floor, trying to still his shuddering body, and the scream that left his lips showed no signs of abating…

…and then he was through. The blade stuck the floor and he let go of it, the switch automatically disengaging as his fingers released it. He fell back, pain and nausea filling his shaking body and the urge to vomit rising within him. He was so cold, his sweat icy against his skin, and he just wanted to lie back, but his mind was urging him on now.

Stop the bleeding…. you've got to stop the bleeding!

He opened his eyes woozily. He was lightheaded and dizzy, trying to brace himself for what he would see. He was covered in blood – his own blood, his mind reminded him, accompanied by the sudden urge to vomit.

He dragged himself weakly across the floor with clumsy hands. His heart was pounding and his stomach churned as he tried not to think about the amount of blood that was pumping out of him, tried to focus only on what he needed to do to stay alive. The room around him appeared to be growing darker.

"Come on, you can do this," he whispered.

Who are you kidding? A small voice in his mind whispered back mockingly. *You've had it. Lost too much blood – lost half of your leg as well. You're not getting out of this one.*

Closing his eyes he forced as much strength as he could muster from his body. Then he felt them – dozens of red hot points, like needles boring into his skin – all across both legs, chest and arms, and looking down his eyes widened in hopeless horror. Whilst the bulk of the creature had fallen away with the portion of his leg that he had cut free, part of it must have shifted upwards into the path of the blade as he had cut – but instead of killing it, it had in fact sprayed tiny portions of it into the air along with his blood and severed tissue. Those tiny specks of matter were now growing and spreading like some kind of corrosive external cancer on the surface of his body. Instead of the one large mass on his leg, he now had dozens all over him.

"No..." he whimpered, sagging back against the bulkhead. "It's not fair..."

There was a faint slithering from all around him now as the other creatures moved toward him, sensing a potential food source.

There's no walking away from this one, he told himself. A crazed urge to laugh seized him. It quickly soured, replaced with a wave of hopeless and hollow fear.

This was death, plain and simple.

His life had never been anything particularly special. He hadn't created works of art, written books or music, nor had he achieved any great scientific or humanitarian goals to be proud of. His days had been simple – a tedious job culminating in an evening spent drinking with friends in a smoky bar down on some godforsaken colony or finding his latest fleeting conquest amongst the lonely women that wandered in seeking companionship. He was leaving behind no legacy, and no children – and only a string of past lovers to remember him by. Yet despite it all his mind still fought desperately for life and a way to escape from this situation, and stubbornly refused to believe this was it. Death was something that happened to others – other people who weren't him. How could he die? He was the centre of his own universe.

Blinding white lights burst across his field of vision. He no longer registered any pain. His mind and body were shutting down, numb from shock as nature mercifully spared him from the agony at the last. The other creatures had reached him now, swarming onto his body and melting his flesh into soup and burrowing deep into his body with their burning tendrils.

And through it all, that terrible guttural chant – that unearthly summons – resonated around him, no longer broadcasting just from the speakers, echoing from out of the structure of the station itself as though it had been transformed into a metal womb that was now giving birth to some blasphemous form of life.

*

The science vessel docked two hours later and a small team made their way into the cramped confines of the relay. They reported that the station appeared to be deserted, but playing some garbled transmission. There was no sign of the technician who had been assigned to repair the station's systems, only a few curious items scattered across the floor – metal buttons, a watch, a belt buckle and so on. There was also no sign of any kind of contaminant, despite the report they had received indicating it was 'everywhere'.

None of them saw the pale mass of roiling tissue, now covered in a protective skin of scales and having fully united all the scattered parts of itself, that was edging silently along the outside of the docking tube toward the hull of the science vessel.

Whilst through the dark and icy void of space, unnoticed by most that had the means to detect or sense the signal, the call continued on: an endless and secret summons.

A summons which, by accident, had finally been answered.

Draystone's Secret

There had always been unsettling rumours connected to the old Draystone building, but I doubt anybody ever could have guessed the truth about it. I certainly couldn't have, and wish I still counted myself amongst the ignorant. It's been just over six months now since I got out of that place, and thinking back still brings a cold terror over me and a nervous tremor to my hands. The building itself, a large old bookshop with the words DRAYSTONE'S in faded gold writing against a dusty green background, looked unassuming and run-down from the outside. It sat on a quiet corner of Savernake Avenue in the old part of town, and was the sort of place most visitors passed by without ever noticing. Inside, the floor above the shop was a sprawling warren of winding linoleum hallways and doors to numerous apartments, all nestled beneath sagging ceilings speckled with damp spots, filled with an air of age and general neglect. An oddly disquieting place, it comprised too many strange corners, odd angles and awkward steps in random places, as though the structure somehow had been deviously co-designed by H. P. Lovecraft and M. C. Escher.

I knew it well, having had the dubious fortune of being the lone tenant for the past nine months. That hadn't always been the case: others had come and gone in my entire three years there, but nobody stayed long. Whether it was the single shared toilet, the damp and leaky ceilings, the bad wiring or just the odd atmosphere, I couldn't say. But it seemed I was always returning home up that narrow staircase to find another room vacant, and Draystone moving silently through it like a ghost, readying it for a new tenant.

Draystone himself was a strange man, thin and gaunt, with pale haunted eyes and a distinctive limp in his left leg. You could hear him creaking his way slowly up from the shop below sometimes. He seemed lonely and distant, and gazed through you when speaking. I had heard a few things about him before moving in: how he had lost his whole family in a terrible house fire years before, that he was a devoutly religious man, though nobody ever saw him at church, and that he had become something of a strange recluse in the past few years. But it wasn't until two days after I had moved in that a neighbour had revealed a darker side to the history.

"Don't you know?" she said, a bright conspiratorial spark in her eyes as she leaned against the doorway of her room. "Apparently, his wife had a breakdown, so they say. She went completely insane. Years of abuse, or something like that. Anyway, the story goes that she tied all the children to chairs around the dining room table and torched the place, herself with it."

"That's horrible."

"They say it was her final act of revenge against him."

"Does he really seem *that* bad, Lorraine?" I folded my arms, trying to reconcile my impressions of the man with the character she was describing. "I mean, you've been here a while now, right?"

"Four months or so, and I don't know," she shrugged, "there's something odd about him. Not sure all the screws are in tight, if you get me. He makes me squirm. And then there's *the room*." She lowered her voice and gestured down the hallway. I followed her gaze but saw only the turn in the corridor. "Follow that along, go past all the other rooms, and you'll come to a door all alone at the very end of the hall."

"And?" I prompted.

"He never rents that room out, and nobody lives there. But every now and then, always at night, you'll hear people sneaking in there. It's not just the same people either, as far as I can tell from the voices – but it's always couples," she added with a wink.

"You're pulling my leg."

"Give it a few nights, you'll see. I call it the *sex room*."

I was staring down the hallway in surprise, and glanced back at her.

"It's not often I'm lost for words."

"I know, odd right? He won't let unmarried couples live here, and always wears a cross, yet he has that going on up here."

We were interrupted by the uneven tread of heavy shoes creaking their way up the old narrow stairs. Lorraine shot me a wickedly impish grin and slipped back into her room. I returned to mine, making a mental note to catch up with her again and find out more. But I never got the chance. Three days later she was gone, her room empty when I trudged home from a tedious day at the office, and Draystone was quietly surveying it, as though scrutinising every speck of dust and mark on the wall. He turned and watched me as I searched for the key to my door.

"Mr Jameson," he acknowledged softly. Watching me from the doorway in his dark suit, gaunt faced locked in a motionless gaze, he was the epitome of silent menace, and I fought hard to get the image of an undertaker out of my head.

"Please, call me Michael." I pointed at the empty room. "Has Lorraine gone?"

"Moved out this morning," he nodded, fingering the small silver cross that hung around his neck. "Gone to look after her mother, I believe."

"She never said she was leaving," I still pretended to look for my keys, though in reality I had them hidden in my hand. I seldom got to speak with Draystone – rarely wanted to in truth – but Lorraine had seemed settled here, and I was curious to find out more.

"Short notice," Draystone said, then turned and limped away towards the stairs without another word. It was a year before he got another tenant in the room next to mine.

That was the strange thing about the whole situation, Draystone certainly didn't need to rent out any of these rooms on the upper floor. He clearly wasn't short of money, and the rent he asked for was so ridiculously low he must actually have been making a loss from it.

I had the cheapest room in the whole place – but also one of the largest, with a ceiling that bowed alarmingly, a floor that was less than level, a window that didn't lock or shut properly and an intrusive CCTV camera fixed to the building opposite that looked right into my flat as it surveyed the street. I didn't mind too much, it actually made me feel a bit better about the dodgy window, since my landlord seemed in no hurry to fix it. I had considered asking to move into one of the other rooms, but they were all a lot smaller, so I decided just to grin and bear it. I was, after all, saving a small fortune by living there.

The strange couples came and went throughout my three years tenancy. I would hear them in the evenings, at least once a week, whispering and giggling as they scurried down that twisting hallway to the lone door at the far end. In time, I kind of stopped noticing them. And one by one the tenants all moved on, until I alone remained with the whole floor of locked empty rooms, and the strange nocturnal visitors, all to myself. It wasn't long before I forgot how bizarre the whole set-up was, it slipped into normality, that curious mix of tedium and comfortable familiarity that very quickly becomes your everyday world. I busied myself with work, multiple attempts to salvage my ailing love life, and a determined effort to resurrect some progress with my paintings during the evenings. A local gallery had shown some interest in displaying some of them, but I had allowed myself to let my passion slip into a mere hobby, and was finding it harder than I expected to scrape the rust of several years away.

And that was how I made the final discovery about that mysterious room at the end of the hall, on a stormy September night, when the pattering of the rain against the ill-fitting window and a nasty bout of insomnia had threatened to drive me to distraction. So I kicked off the covers, put on some Fleetwood Mac, and armed with a paintbrush, a pack of cigarettes and a good supply of cold gin and tonic, I determined to paint myself to sleep or greet the dawn with a screaming hangover and a finished canvas.

I had just taken a long drag on the third cigarette, paintbrush poised in hand, and was exhaling slowly as if searching for inspiration in the smoke, when there was a heavy thud from somewhere outside my door, hard enough to shake it.

I paused the CD, cutting Stevie Nicks off in mid-flow, a crime for which I vowed someone would be made to pay, and listened for a moment. For a second there was only silence, and then another weighty thud and a strange sound, like a bizarre mix between a choking cough and a whimper. Then I remembered the mysterious couples that came and went to the sex room.

Keep it down you two, I sighed, reaching out for the CD remote. But something stayed my hand. I had never heard noises that like before, and instinctively knew something wasn't right. I walked to my door and pressed my ear against it, holding my breath, but the hallway beyond was silent now. Gently, I slid the lock on my door and peered out. All seemed still and normal, and I was about to turn back when I noticed something glint on the edge of the rectangle of light thrown by my open doorway.

It was an earring.

I quickly located a pair of jeans and a crumpled t-shirt before making my way back out, flicking on the dim hall light as I did. The hallway was always cold at night, even in summer, and the weak bulb only served to showcase the many nooks and shadows that surrounded me – too many doorways and alcoves for comfort. The place was a mugger's paradise. I shivered as I walked quietly over and picked up the lone item of jewellery. It was partially crushed and twisted, as though it had been torn out and trodden on. My curiosity getting the better of me, I followed the corridor all the way around to the sex room.

The door was ajar.

The whole time I had lived there, I had never seen it open or even unlocked. I had often wondered just how Draystone advertised it and how he passed on the keys – not that I had any interest in using it, only that I didn't know of anyone outside the former tenants who had heard about it.

The lure of seeing inside, even for a second, was too much to resist. The door swung inwards at my touch, revealing a lone double-bed sitting in the middle of a room with a thick cream carpet and white-painted woodchip walls. Dark red curtains hung over the windows, and a box of batteries lay tipped on its side on the floor next to an open tube of cherry-flavoured lubricant. Clothes, both male and female, were strewn clumsily on the floor, and the bed sheets were crumpled and twisted. The smell of sweat and passion was heavy on the air, mingled with a faint whiff of perfume. I moved closer to the bed as I looked around, disappointed that it was so plainly decorated. After all I had heard of it, I had half imagined whips, chains and a glistening PVC gimp suit to be hanging down from the walls. The only curious object in the room was a strange kind of copper funnel that was set in the middle of the ceiling. It looked more than a little out of place, and had no obvious function that I could discern. It was then that I remembered that I hadn't heard anyone leave, and suddenly felt uncomfortably voyeuristic. I tried to tell myself that I hadn't done anything too terrible by sneaking in here. It wasn't like I had actually tried to spy on anyone in the midst of carnal passion. But my conscience was kicking in and I knew I should get out fast before somebody came back.

As I turned to leave there was a faint creak from behind me, and I realised that a small section of the wall had come away from the rest. It was only when I reached out and the whole panel shifted, that I understood it was a concealed doorway.

I really should have got out then, and I knew it. Should have turned tail and retreated to my room at these bizarre signs. I've seen and laughed at enough horror movies where people blunder stupidly ahead instead of turning back, but a perverse curiosity had taken hold and compelled me to move forward, instead of heeding the voice of reason and sanity. Besides, this was reality and not some cheesy Hollywood flick. My heart was in my throat as I pulled the door open, knowing at any second I might be discovered, but that made this all the more enticing somehow. Beyond the doorway, a flight of steps rose steeply up into darkness past a wall of bare brick, and I climbed them as quietly as possible. The steps underfoot were polished from use and free of dust, and I stopped when my hand ran out of banister, allowing my eyes to adjust. Gradually, I realised I was standing in a narrow attic hallway that stretched down past two padlocked doors to a third at the far end which was partly open and spilled a narrow strip of light across the floor.

I hesitated then, common sense marching back and ordering me to turn around and go back to my room before I was discovered and evicted. I was about to obey, when from that door at the end of the hall there issued a terrified shriek, followed by what could only have been a sudden choked-off gasp and abrupt silence.

Genuine fear finally seized me then, standing in the darkness, heart beating, staring at the steps that would take me back down to my room as I wondered what to do. I should have slinked away, crept back to my normal life and shut this unusual strangeness out. But I couldn't. I had gone too far and seen too much, and curiosity burned within me as strongly as my fear. But I would have been lying if I didn't also admit to a growing sense of guilt. If somebody was hurt or in pain beyond that door, how could I just turn away and leave them to suffer?

My hands and legs physically shook as I walked down that passageway, treading lightly. In the back of my mind was the notion that I might just be about to intrude on some strange kind of twisted sex game, but I knew that this was something darker and more serious.

I peered gingerly around the door into a large attic cluttered with old bed frames and mattresses, strange glass bottles, boxes of assorted junk, and other items of furniture shrouded in dust-sheets. It was as though a mad hoarder had been accumulating items from house clearances. But a clear path ran through the middle of it all, and the attic branched off to the right up ahead, following the odd shape of the building. As I made my way forward, I noticed the pungent stench of formaldehyde in the air, and as I rounded the corner and the rest of the attic opened up before me, I stopped in shock at the sight that met my eyes.

Ahead of me, sitting around a long ornate dining table and looking for all the world like a demented mannequin's tea-party, were the preserved remains of several of the previous tenants. They stared sightlessly down upon their empty china plates, glasses and silver cutlery, their mouths twisted into grisly smiles with wire, and strange symbols were daubed on their flesh in long-dried blood. I baulked as I recognised Lorraine's corpse among them. There were a few unoccupied chairs, but even these had place settings prepared before them. Resting in the middle of the table was a large milky crystal, covered with the same curious glyphs that were daubed onto the bodies. It sat within a crudely made copper dish which also bore the same bizarre markings and which had a long tube that extended down through the table and into the floor below.

On the floor next to the table lay a young woman. She was dressed only in her underwear, and her body was spattered in blood. There was a ragged tear to one of her earlobes, a deep gash on her forehead, and red marks on her throat revealed where she had been strangled. Near to her, their hands almost touching, lay a young man, also dressed only in his underwear, the side of his head bloody and bruised.

It felt like I stood there for hours, staring in shock and disbelief at that macabre scene, though it could only have been seconds. I can still see them now, every detail, etched vividly into my mind whenever I close my eyes. What snapped me away from that awful sight was the sudden realisation that one of the dust sheets off to my right was moving, just in the periphery of my vision. As I turned to look, something slammed heavily against the side of my head. I hit the floor, and everything went dark.

*

"Welcome to the family."

The voice that spoke was all-too familiar, and I opened my eyes groggily to see Draystone watching me. He was sitting in one of the previously unoccupied dining chairs across the table from me, holding a long hypodermic needle in his thin fingers. I tried to stand up, but ropes bit into my arms and legs.

"I wanted to wait until you were awake. It seemed only fair."

"Come near me and I'll scream," I warned him, hoping the tremor in my voice wasn't too apparent.

He laughed at that. "Go ahead and scream – others have. The building is old and the walls are thick, and at this time of night anyone sober enough to care is home in bed."

"Please! For God's sake, don't do this!"

"God?" he laughed, reaching for the silver cross around his neck. "I wear this to remind me of what I once was, what I once believed in." He stood up and moved around the table towards me, the needle glinting in his grasp. "But where was God when my wife stole my family from me? Where was God when I screamed and prayed for a miracle until I was hoarse?"

I shook my head, tears stinging my eyes and fear crippling my tongue.

"Nowhere," he hissed as he crouched beside me. "I gave him devotion, and he gave me nothing but ashes and grief."

I tried to speak but no sound came out. My arms and legs were shaking now, and my heart threatened to explode from my chest.

"But you know what?" he whispered, leaning in close, the glinting needle tip easing in toward my eye. I tried to flinch away but Draystone's hand shot around to the back of my head, holding it in place. His breath assaulted my skin as he leaned in, and I squirmed as the needle drew closer. "There are other powers in this world. Beings so old we no longer have names for them, but they are still here. They were more than willing to help."

He drew back, taking the needle away, but this brought no relief. I twisted my hands against my bonds and strained my arms and legs without making it obvious what I was trying to do.

"Do you know what they revealed to me?" he continued, a wry smile on his lips as his gaze turned to the crystal. "The solution was all around me, bound up in something I once deemed sinful and unclean. How blind I was."

He turned and gave me a sideways glance, and I knew he was daring me to guess. But I could only shake my head.

"Sex," he laughed. "Of all the things."

My right arm was slowly working loose, a mix of sweat and my frantic wrenching and twisting.

"Sex has a power, and it has energy. Oh, you wouldn't believe what that energy can do if you tap into it. It's potent and regenerative. It's pure life energy, filled with that spark of creation and passion. It is that magical moment when life moves from a potential to a reality." He ran a hand gently over the large crystal in the middle of the table. "This is right above the bed below, and all that life energy is directed right up into it. And when I have enough stored up, I can bring them back. I can channel back the spirits of my family into these empty vessels of flesh and bone and bind them there with life energy. It takes years to get enough to bring back so many – but soon I will be with my children again, and I shall settle a very old score with my wife."

"You're crazy," I finally whispered, my voice hoarse. "Totally mad."

"But these two," he shot a disdainful glance down at the body of the prostitute and the young man lying in a heap at his feet, "were like you." He gestured at me with the needle, then angled it to point at Lorraine's corpse as well. "You all couldn't leave well enough alone. Had to go peeking and snooping where you weren't meant to, and saw what was private. But it doesn't matter – spare vessels are always useful."

"I've got friends, and family," I said quickly. "People who'll come looking for me!"

"You don't think she did too?" he nodded at Lorraine. "They all did. But did you see anything in the papers? Did the police come asking questions?"

"No," I whispered, a chilling realisation suddenly dawning on me. There had been nothing – no investigations, no questions, no news stories.

"The ones I summon, those forgotten ones I discovered, are very good at making sure people forget the things I want them to. You'll be forgotten too, just as they all were."

The rope around my right hand was working loose, and the chair was on the verge of giving out too, probably riddled with woodworm, but I feared moving too much while he was looking at me, and I was already afraid that the beads of sweat on my face and brow might give the game away. My mind raced, desperately trying to find some way out of this – from the cutlery on the table that might serve as a crude weapon, to wondering how heavy and solid that crystal might be if I swung it against his head.

And then the young man on the floor stirred – his arm lifted and his eyes flickered open, and I held my breath, terrified that he might make a sound and draw Draystone's attention.

"You're forgetting," I said quickly, hoping to keep Draystone's gaze fixed on me, my voice trembling, "the bodies here – they're older than your children would have been."

"I don't care about the shells," he waved a hand dismissively, "only the souls within. The body is just flesh. They will be my children whatever their outward form might be."

"But how will you know it's really them? How…"

Draystone shot forward then, the needle glinting toward my face once more. "I think you need to be *quiet* now!" he hissed, his eyes blazing furiously as I recoiled from him. Then he blinked and looked down at the needle in his hand, and a faint smile flickered over his thin lips. "Now, where were we?"

From behind Draystone there was movement as the young man rose shakily to his feet, then slammed into the back of his attacker with a cry of rage. At the same time Draystone pitched forward and the needle flew from his grasp and struck the surface of the table next to me.

Without stopping to see what happened next, I did the only thing that I could think of – I pushed with my feet as hard as I could, tipping the old chair up on the back legs, then let it slam down against the floor whilst trying to keep the back of my head from hitting along with it. The shock was still jarring and I failed to keep my head from smacking against the floorboards as I struck. But I heard the chair break at the same time, and the bonds loosened a little, and I rolled onto my side as I managed to pull one arm free, my head ringing.

I could hear the sounds of a struggle behind me, but couldn't see what was happening – my legs were still coiled in rope and one of my hands was still bound tightly at the wrist. I clawed and tugged at my bonds. Finally, they gave way.

I staggered to my feet to see the two men wrestling with each other over the table. The young man had one hand around my landlord's throat and the other clamped around his head, whilst Draystone himself was struggling to reach the needle that was rolling across the table just out of reach of his fingers. Then he changed tactics, and drove his elbow back into the young man's stomach, before lunging again for the needle.

But he hadn't seen me. In a panic I snatched up the hypodermic – and as he turned I stabbed wildly at him with it, a cry of anger and horror bursting from my lips.

It plunged straight into his left eye.

Draystone froze, his jaw dropping open in surprise as he stared at me with his right eye. He was trying to blink.

I think the look of horror on his face must have mirrored that on my own. I jumped back, and then everything seemed to happen in slow motion. Draystone swayed like a tree in a storm, pawing ineffectually at the needle embedded in his eye with trembling hands - then he crashed down onto the table as his legs buckled under him, and I heard the awful sickening crunch as the hypodermic went fully in as his face slammed against the tabletop. For a second his whole body trembled and twitched, and he desperately reached for something with his right arm. His shuddering fingers fumbled at the milky crystal – and then he just went still, his hand coming to rest atop it.

I also went still, staring in mute horror at the sight before me.

What have I done?

A hand touched my shoulder. The young man was watching me, his hair matted with blood and his face pale and frightened.

"Are you ok?" he asked, his voice as unsteady as mine had been earlier. I nodded, but I didn't trust myself to say anything. Then he saw the woman lying on the floor and knelt beside her, touching her face with a trembling hand.

"Oh God."

I just watched blankly as he closed her dead eyes. It didn't even feel real to me – it was like watching events on a screen. I just stood there, staring.

"Can you move?" he said at last, looking up at me. "Let's get the hell out of here and call the police."

"Yes," I managed finally. "Yes, we should."

I dimly remembering following him down out of that attic space, pausing only to allow him to get dressed before making our way through the twisting hallway of the building that I had once called home. It all felt different now, unfamiliar and unwelcoming, and I wondered how I had ever allowed myself to stay there. How had I let all those little odd occurrences over the years become so familiar and normal?

We called the police from my mobile phone, standing in a shop doorway across the street from the old bookshop. I couldn't face going back into my room, not just yet. And I wondered what would happen when those cars with their wailing sirens finally drew up. I had just killed a man – and the worst part was, I didn't know if I had meant to or not. It had all happened so fast, and I had acted instead of thinking. I wasn't sure looking back just what I had intended to do with that needle – had I really meant to aim it for his face, or just to scare him back? The fact that Draystone had been a killer and had planned to murder me didn't seem to make what I had done any less terrible.

The police arrived soon after, cordoning off the road as they went into the house and we were taken away to the station. To be honest, most of what happened after was a blur. All I could see was Draystone's face with that needle sticking out of it, and I kept hearing that awful sound over and over as his face struck the table. I must have been half out of my mind with guilt and shock. It was only some time later, while I was anxiously making my confession down at the station, and seeing looks of confusion on the faces of the officers there, that I learned they hadn't found Draystone's body in that attic, nor had there been any sign of the milky crystal we had described to them. They did, however, find the corpses around the table just as we had reported, with my landlord's fingerprints all over them, along with enough taxidermy equipment to preserve several elephants.

The story was in the papers for weeks, and with it came the overdue outcry from friends and relatives of Lorraine and the rest of the victims – as though they had somehow just resurfaced in their memories. I don't pretend to understand it, and the more I think about it, the less I feel able to sleep at night.

They never found Draystone, despite an ongoing manhunt. Sometimes I wonder just how he survived, and how he's managed to elude capture these past six months. And I keep thinking about what he said about finding older forces that were willing to aid him.

Barrie, the young man who escaped that attic with me, kept in touch following that awful night. He was the only one who knew what truly happened, and he was a great support in helping me through my ongoing grief and guilt, just as I know he appreciated having someone who understood what he had been through. It was funny how that horrible event changed us both, turned two strangers into the closest of friends.

Barrie even managed to shed some light on just what had happened that night, and the look on his face as he recounted it to me has never left my memory since.

"I found out about it on Craigslist, good place for a hookup, apparently," he'd confessed over coffee one afternoon, the drone of traffic outside forming a comforting backdrop of normality against memories of a night that was anything but. "I met her across the street outside. Said she had a deal with the landlord, and had the keys to the room. I thought the place looked like a dump, but she was hot, so what did I care? Anyway, it was all going great until we found that staircase. I guess he hadn't shut it properly. We thought we'd check it out, for a laugh, but he was up there – sitting at that table, watching that crystal. When he realised we'd seen those bodies, he went crazy. I tried to stop him, and that's all I remember until I woke with a splitting headache to see him coming at you with that needle."

But everything changed three nights ago. I had just got in from work and flicked on the news when I saw the report. Barrie had been found dead in his home, just across town from where I now live. He had been tied to a chair in his kitchen, with strange marks daubed in blood on his body and his left eye gouged out. The truly strange thing is police have no idea how the killer got inside the property – there was no sign of forced entry or any damage to the house. I must have watched that report over and over again as the news repeated it throughout the evening. I couldn't believe what I was seeing. It still doesn't seem real.

I try to tell myself it wasn't a message for me, and that I'm not now in terrible danger. Sometimes I can almost make myself believe it.

Most of the time I know full well that Draystone was just plain crazy. Just a lonely old man lost to his own mad delusions. But other times, usually just after dusk when the character of the world changes and those things that seem laughable by day suddenly take on a different, more solid reality, I sit inside, afraid to go near the windows for fear he might be standing outside, a knife or needle in one hand and that milky crystal in the other, and I wonder.

Thornway Hollow

Two men stepped into the silent stillness, torch beams lancing the darkness and playing across narrow hallways covered with flaking paint and over a floor strewn with litter and rubble - discarded fragments of tile, wood and broken glass. Dust motes hung thickly in the air, and the brooding silence was broken only by the breathing of the men, and the occasional creak and groan from somewhere deep within the heart of the old building.

"Here, take this." The first man handed his torch to his colleague as he slipped the rucksack from his shoulders and carefully removed a small video camera.

"Figured they'd have tightened security by now." The second man glanced out through the open door at the starless dark of the night and the stretch of overgrown uneven lawn they had just darted across. "Lucky they never fixed that break in the fence."

"Come on, Tony," his colleague laughed as he switched on the camera and activated the light at the front of it, "there's nothing here worth taking."

"True," he passed the torch back. "So where first, Mark?"

"The morgue and the chapel, and then we'll work outwards from there. I want to try and get over into the south wing as well if we can. I think there might be a way through the underground tunnels."

"What's in the south wing?" Tony frowned, fishing a small rectangular device from his pack and switching it on. On the tiny screen a temperature and EMF reading flickered into life.

"There was a big fire there, right around the time this place was shut. A few nurses and patients died in it. If we want to find ghosts, well, traumatic deaths tend to leave traces."

Together they moved down the long hallway, passing boarded up exterior windows and pushing through creaking interior doors with shattered glass panels, footsteps scrunching and crunching noisily on the debris underfoot as their lights danced across broken glass and illuminated the black recesses of side rooms.

Around them the once-venerable corridors and steep crumbling stairwells of Thornway Hollow Sanatorium stretched out in eerie emptiness, wearing a grimy and desolate shroud of decay and neglect that the long years of closure and abandonment had gifted with abundance. The sanatorium itself was actually a series of five large buildings linked by a network of underground passageways and set amidst an overgrown chaos of trees, bushes and tall grasses that were once gentle lawns and landscaped gardens. And like all such institutions, especially those that had been derelict for some time, legends of ghosts and strange activity abounded. The security huts at the two main gates, and the many prominent "beware of the dogs" signs posted there were meant to deter the curious or those who had come to steal and vandalise, but in truth had little effect on those who were truly determined to get inside, as the state of the buildings testified.

"Wonder what this place was like before," Tony mused, pulling a flap of flaking paint off the wall. "Do you think the spirits can see this? Or do they just see it as it was?"

"Depends if the haunting is residual, an echo caught in time - or intelligent, an actual aware presence," Mark explained. "Even then, I believe there are some that aren't even aware they are dead. Then you have those spirits that know exactly what they are, and see the world as it is, but are unable to rest for whatever reason."

"And those are the ones you try to help?"

"If they'll listen, and if they want to be helped. Too many people treat intelligent haunting sites like some kind of sideshow attraction. They forget that these are still living spirits that are trapped."

Tony let the peeling paint fall to the floor and turned his attention back to the readings he had been taking.

"How's it looking?" Mark cast a glance at Tony. With his dark clothing it almost appeared as if his head were moving without a body, but then he stepped around into the light at the front of the camera.

"Steady so far. No significant temperature changes or cold spots. No EMF either."

"Watch out up ahead," Mark cautioned, his eye returning to the viewer of the video camera. "There's a big hole in the floor. Don't forget what happened last time."

"Hey, I saw it," Tony bristled, shooting an annoyed glance at the camera.

"You almost went straight in," Mark smiled. "Too busy staring at your readings, as I recall."

Tony waved a hand dismissively, but took great care to step around the hole as they came to it all the same. It was deep, and flooded with murky water and filled with floating debris, some clearly very old, and others – crushed and half submerged beer cans and bottles – less so. "Looks like somebody's been having a party here."

"Tell me about it," Mark gestured at a nearby wall covered with a scrawl of graffiti. "That wasn't here last time, either."

"We're in the wrong jobs," Tony laughed. "We should get hired as a guard here. They don't seem to actually do anything."

"Lucky for us," Mark reminded him.

They moved deeper in, past murky reception hatches festooned with cobwebs and narrow side rooms that were mostly missing their doors, with rotting beds and festering mattresses still in place within. In one was some kind of rusted surgical device beside one of the beds, but time had rendered it unidentifiable. In the next was a smashed toilet still fixed in place, shattered shards of yellowing tile and flaked plaster covering the floor, along with fragments of an old porcelain sink. While from another a small brown bat shot suddenly out of the doorway as they shone their lights inside, causing them both to jump as it fluttered down the hallway.

"This place looks even worse than it did six months ago," Mark muttered, noting that there was now not a single window that hadn't been smashed, or an electrical box that hadn't been torn open and robbed for parts and wiring. He also noted more crushed beer cans, cigarette stubs and a few cleaner mattresses in some of the rooms. "Squatters?" he suggested.

"Crack-heads more likely," Tony frowned, checking the floor warily for used needles. "Or kids getting high and screwing out here. I think the guards at the gate have stopped caring. It's only that this place is supposed to be listed that keeps them from tearing it down."

"Who's got the cash to fix it up?" Mark sighed. "And who'd want to?"

They moved through another set of internal doors, the floor creaking and flexing unnervingly in places under their shoes, and the flaking walls streaked with moisture stains. In this part of the building the boards had been ripped away from the shattered outside windows, and the rain and the elements had left their mark clearly, as had the heaps of wind-blown leaves that littered the floor.

"Looks like this place has been under water." Mark panned the camera across the walls. Even the graffiti here was wearing off as the paint crumbled under it. He could just make out a few random scrawls – parts of names, messages that somebody "woz ere", and the word "LEAVE" scrawled in some kind of black ink in large letters across one part of the wall. He turned the camera back onto the hallway, keeping his eyes peeled for any glimpses of shadow figures, or light anomalies that might indicate the presence of a spirit.

"Here's the chapel," Tony remarked as they approached a warped set of double wooden doors. The dusty glass panels set into them were unbroken and the faintest outline of a gold cross could be seen etched on each. "May as well start here then go down to the morgue?"

"Yeah, go for it," Mark nodded. "We didn't get much time in here last visit."

The doors opened with a groaning shriek as rusting hinges were forced to move once more, and torchlight flooded into a room that had not seen anything but shadows for a long time. The stale air stank of dampness, mould and mildew. The rows of disintegrating pews lining the room were thick with dust and cobwebs, and a leaning lectern still sat at the far end. The paint on the walls hung in tattered strips, and the faint dripping of moisture echoed from the back of the room.

"Get some stills," Mark suggested, as he finished sweeping the camera slowly around and moved to respectfully straighten an old crucifix still mounted to the far wall. "See if we get anything."

"Stay over there so I can get you in too," Tony gestured at a spot near the lectern as he unhooked a small digital camera from his belt.

The flash exploded with light, flooding the room with brightness in quick succession as Tony worked his way around it.

He got half way when the chapel doors slammed shut.

The two men turned instantly, flashlights flaring through the gloom and picking out the doors.

"Could have been a draught?" Tony ventured, his heart thumping.

"Would take a lot to slam those, and the air in here is still," Mark reasoned. He lifted the video camera up to his eye and filmed as he approached the doors. "If there is a spirit here with us," he said loudly, "we mean you no harm or disrespect. Please, show us that you are here. Move these doors for us again."

Nothing happened, and Tony checked the readings on the temperature in the room.

He shook his head. "No change."

"If anyone is with us, please, let us know you are here. Show us you are here."

After a few minutes of silence Mark reached out and opened the doors himself, the hinges shrieking once again as they swung open. "It was just the breeze coming in from outside. A broken window or something."

"Maybe." Tony didn't sound convinced.

"This place has been abandoned for close to ten years. It's full of holes."

"Yeah, but I'm not feeling a breeze here."

"Let's move on anyway," Mark suggested. "We've a lot more ground to cover, and I think we'll get more activity downstairs."

Tony held up his digital voice recorder. "What about trying to catch some EVPs?"

"Not here," Mark shook his head, and Tony detected the tiniest trace of irritation in his voice. "I really want to get down to the morgue."

"What is it with you and morgues?" Tony sighed. "You know, this is not a healthy obsession."

Mark shot him a look of weary amusement. "I don't have an obsession. We both know they're usually hotspots of activity, and last time we never even got down there, because of Jenny."

"I already said sorry about bringing her," Tony explained as they moved out into the hall. "I didn't know she was going to scream at every single little thing."

"You know she went and set her own group up?" Mark scowled. "With that friend of hers - Ian, the one who thinks he's a medium. Medium intelligence, more like."

"I'd say even that's pushing it. He needs a manual just to figure out how to wipe his ass. It was funny though, when she accused you of being a Zak Bagans wannabe," Tony chuckled, then fell swiftly silent when he caught Mark's glare.

"Moving on," Mark muttered softly, gesturing ahead with the torch.

They descended a narrow staircase, shoulders and elbows rubbing flakes from the walls as they moved and the steps groaning faintly under them. The door at the bottom was different to the rest they had seen – sturdier and made of white-painted metal. But someone had scrawled the word "LEAVE" across it in what looked like dried mud.

"Encouraging sign," Tony smiled. "Do we leave?"

Mark gave him a sideways glance as he pulled the door open. "Yes, because we came all this way to run at a message left by some kids."

"That's what I thought."

The hallway they emerged into was wider than the last, with heavy windowless walls and a solid concrete floor. The rotting metal skeleton of an old hospital bed loomed out of the gloom in the middle of the passageway as their torches beat back the shadows, and they squeezed past it. Mark again with his eye glued to the video camera and Tony checking the temperature.

"It's colder down here," he remarked.

"Could just be that we've gone below ground level," Mark cautioned. "Let's see what happens as we get deeper in."

"This place stinks," Tony wrinkled his nose as they walked on, his eyes watching the temperature reading as it steadily dropped. "Guess there's no supply of fresh air getting in here."

"At least we can rule out draughts."

"I just hope we don't stumble onto a body or anything down here. That would freak me out more than any ghost. Imagine if we came across some dead homeless-"

"Hold it!" Mark stopped so abruptly that Tony had to turn and double-back.

"What?"

He held up the video camera. "Battery just went dead."

"I thought you charged it yesterday?"

"I did."

Somewhere in the deep darkness ahead of them a door slammed loudly.

Their hearts quickened.

"Where did that come from?"

"The morgue, I think," Mark said, a faint smile crossing his face.

Tony rolled his eyes.

They made their way silently forward as their torches glinted on pools of stagnant water that had gathered in the recesses of the corridor and shone on droplets dripping from the ceiling. Their hearts were hammering fast and despite the growing chill, Tony was hot and uncomfortable. But the adrenaline was surging too, and his sense of fear was coupled with a nervous excitement – but he forced himself to keep a calm head. It would be too easy to let his imagination get the better of him. Too easy to let himself see what he wanted to see, instead of staying rational and considering the possible mundane explanations for things first. But it was hard not to. Unlike Mark, he had only been ghost-hunting for just over four months, though he had harboured a fascination for most of his life, and had only caught a few tantalising glimpses that hinted at the existence of spirits walking unseen amongst the living. Mark had been at this game for a couple of years, and had stories that could chill the blood about things he had witnessed – shadow figures flitting down hallways, disembodied voices calling his name, doors opening and closing by themselves, poltergeist activity hurling pots and cups furiously around a kitchen, and strange glowing wisps caught moving in darkened rooms on night vision cameras while EMF meters spiked and surged.

"The smell's getting worse. And the temperature's really dropping too," Tony whispered as they turned a corner and found themselves staring down another hallway, the few feet of torchlight revealing a concrete floor strewn with old pipes, years of dust and grit, an old ladder - and then darkness ahead and darkness behind, leaving them all alone in a tiny oasis of light. His heart pounded and the hairs on the back of his neck and arms prickled, and he cast a sideways glance at Mark. But if his colleague felt the same sense of nervous fear, it didn't show. Tony wasn't sure if he was just better at hiding it, or if he genuinely was a tough nut to crack, but he envied him either way.

"EMF?"

"None."

"Ok, it should be just down here on the right," Mark whispered, gesturing with the torch. As the light flashed over the wall, they both saw the word "Morgue" picked out in silver reflective writing on a small sign fastened to a heavy metal door. "There."

"Yeah, but – hang on," Tony directed his own torch at it. "Look at that."

Beneath the sign on the door was a second word – it looked like it has been scratched into the paint on the metal: LEAVE.

"Are you sure that's kids doing that?"

"You saw the graffiti and beer cans upstairs. It's just people messing about."

The door to the morgue opened with surprisingly little effort, and surprisingly little noise. They followed the guiding light of their torches down a grimy tile-clad passageway and emerged into a larger open space that was so icy their breath frosted on the air as it left their lips. Against one wall there was a huge row of silver cold chambers, but all but two of the doors were missing.

"Should have brought the night-vision camera," Mark cursed softly.

"Yeah, why didn't you?"

"I put it on charge last night and forgot it wasn't packed," Mark sighed. "Must be getting o-"

From deep in the darkness somewhere further down the hallway another door slammed.

"Shit," Tony craned his neck to look back, but saw only shadows. Suddenly his bladder was uncomfortably full. In the back of his mind a little voice was wondering what they would do if the batteries went in the torches as well. He didn't like the thought of blundering around blindly in this pitch-black maze.

"Ok, get some stills in here, and keep an eye on the EMF readings," Mark suggested, crouching down and rooting around in the rucksack. "I'm going to see if I can find that spare battery."

Tony moved cautiously through the darkness as he explored the other end of the long room, his feet scraping and clattering against the debris underfoot as he lifted the camera. Darkness turned to light for a second as he captured an image of the room, then had to wait as his eyes adjusted after the sudden flare. When his vision returned he checked the image, disappointed not to see any orbs or spectral figures, but intrigued to notice a small doorway in the corner that the shadows had concealed before.

"There's another room back here."

"Be right there," Mark called back, still foraging for the spare battery.

Tony fumbled as he searched for the door handle and finally succeeded in pulling it open. Like the main door to the morgue it opened unusually easily and without a sound, and he found himself stepping into the unknown darkness of a smaller adjoining room. The air in here stank, something sweet and rotten, far worse than any of the mould and mildew from the building above, and he recoiled as something spidery brushed and tickled against the side of his face. He breathed a sigh of relief. It was just an old dead wire hanging down from the ceiling. As he unhooked the torch from his belt and shone the light cautiously around him, he realised this must have been some kind of office. A long row of battered filing cabinets stood against one wall, and close to it a murky water cooler and an old desk that looked buried beneath a pile of debris, dozens of dead flies and accumulated rubbish.

His foot landed in something soft and moist, and the sweet rotten smell suddenly overwhelmed.

With a shiver of revulsion he directed his torch down. His stomach churned at the grisly remains of countless small animals – cats, dogs, bats and squirrels, littering the floor like some kind of nightmarish carpet. Most were festering, in various stages of decomposition, crawling with maggots and barely recognisable. But the few that were fresher bore clear signs of having been gnawed upon – flesh stripped from bones that had been snapped to get at the marrow inside.

His torch flickered as the new batteries struggled and a surge of panic rushed through him. As his lunch from earlier that day made a poor attempt at reincarnation, he turned, blundering almost blindly for the door in his panic. His shaking fingers made four attempts before he finally pulled it open. He was hurrying through, pulse racing and his mind screaming at him to get out, when from out of the corner of his eye he half saw and half sensed movement, and glanced back…

…only to crumple to the floor as something heavy struck the side of his head.

His camera hit the tiled floor with a crack, as did his torch – the light finally fizzling out as it rolled against the wall.

In the middle of the morgue Mark heard the sound and glanced up.

"You ok?" he called, standing slowly and shining his torch at the darkened corner of the room where he knew Tony had been headed. "You trip over something?"

When there was no reply he went to investigate, the light from his torch sweeping across the room. His foot came down on an old light bulb and it shattered like a gunshot. He drew in a sharp intake of breath.

"Shit! Tony?"

The air ahead reeked of decay and rot, and he cupped his hand over his mouth and nose, trying not to gag. Something was up ahead. A dark shape, unmoving, sprawled out on the filthy floor half out of an open doorway.

Another step and he was close enough to recognise it as Tony.

He hurried to his side, hardly feeling the sharp shards of broken tile that bit into his knees as he knelt.

"Tony? Can you hear me?"

He gently shook his friend and relief flooded him as the sprawled form gave a soft moan and stirred. Tony was still clutching his EMF meter in his hand like it was some kind of protective charm, but the screen was dead and lifeless now, totally drained of power.

"What happen-"

But the rest of that sentence was lost underneath the squeaking and crashing as the two remaining doors of the morgue's cold chambers began slamming furiously open and shut behind him as though by some unseen hand.

Reaching into his pocket Mark pulled out the digital voice recorder he carried and activated it. As he did the doors froze, one almost shut and the other wide open, and the room fell silent again.

"Can you hear me?" he asked uneasily. "Can you tell me your name?" he paused, and then: "did you do this to my friend?"

He waited a few seconds, then pressed 'play' and held the speaker close to his ear, hearing his own words echoing back to him.

"Can you hear me? Can you tell me your name? Did you do this to my friend?"

Silence, and then a scratchy female voice – so faint Mark had to strain to hear it – hissed:

"Leave... not... safe!"

"What isn't safe?" Mark asked, pressing 'record' again. "Please, we mean you no harm. We only want to speak with you. To help you."

There was movement behind him, unknown feet crunching and scraping across the floor.

He turned – but before he could fully react two hands hauled him up and back. In the torchlight he caught a glimpse of a man's face, dirty and wild-eyed, staring back at him, flaking lips curled back to reveal blackened teeth gritted in a silent snarl.

Then the wall slammed against his back with such force the torch almost fell from his grip. The face was inches away from his now, staring into his eyes with a crazed fury.

Mark gasped, struggling against the figure pinning him to the wall. It radiated body heat and he knew this was no spirit.

"What - what do you want?" he managed.

The face watching him laughed, a maddened and terrifying sound as spittle foamed from peeling lips and fingers with splintered nails tightened their grip painfully. "Unn-gee!" the man cackled, a thick string of drool running from his lip.

"Hungry?" Mark repeated, his body trembling. He tried to recoil from the man's rank breath, but with the wall against his back there was nowhere to go. "We can bring you food – let us go."

The man released him and Mark readied himself to rush at his attacker. But the man drew a long kitchen knife from his belt with his right hand whilst pulling some strange tarnished metal tags out of the remnants of his soiled clothing with his left. Mark recognised them instantly as pet tags from collars.

"UNN-GEE!" the man declared again as he waved the tags in the air, the knife twisting in his hand as the torchlight glinted on it.

A numbing dread washed over Mark then as he recalled the scandal years ago that had forced the closure of the sanatorium – the fire that had consumed part of the kitchens in the south wing, where the most disturbed and dangerous of the patients had been housed. Dozens of nurses and patients had been trapped and killed, and the fire had been so intense they had found only fragments of some of them. At least three patients had never been accounted for. The whole place had been closed down soon after, but ever since the closure, houses in the vicinity of the sanatorium were always putting up posters for missing cats and dogs. As it all suddenly fell into place, his blood ran cold.

Over on the floor, Tony started to stir, and lifting one hand sluggishly to the back of his head with a faint moan.

The man squealed in eager anticipation at that, eyes gleaming wildly in the torchlight as he span around, lifting the knife.

"Tony!" Mark rushed forward, driving his shoulder into their crazed assailant's back and sending them both crashing to the floor. As they landed, the knife clattered across the floor, and then his head was driven sideways as the man's elbow connected with the side of his face. Reeling, Mark tried to snatch at the knife that lay just out of reach, but with a high-pitched shriek that sounded more like a wounded pig than a human, the man grabbed his head, sharp broken nails slashing skin.

Mark fought back, blindly driving blow after blow into his attacker's body with as much force as he could muster. Blood ran down his stinging face and he twisted his head to the side – anything to keep those splintered nails from tearing into his eyes.

Suddenly the weight that had been pinning him was gone as his attacker lunged for the knife. Mark staggered to his feet, blinking blood from his eyes as his vision blurred.

Got to find a weapon – something…

Then, movement behind him. His heart turned to ice as the man rushed at him, the knife glinting in the torchlight as it lifted, ready to begin flashing down in a lethal arc.

And then his assailant staggered as a length of wood from the floor suddenly impacted against the side of his head, as though thrown by an invisible force. He dropped to the floor as his legs buckled under him, clutching his head with a howl of agony, the knife clattering away across the tiles.

Mark blinked, trying to understand what had happened. The room appeared to be swaying – or was it him?

"Mark?" Tony was sitting up, his face pale and stark with fear. He had a hand cupped over his forehead and there was a deep cut on his cheek where he had hit the floor.

Mark hurried over to him. "We've got to-"

But Tony wasn't looking at him. He was staring at something behind him, and his eyes had gone so wide his pupils seemed lost in an expanse of white.

Mark followed his gaze – and there, in the shaking light of the torch still clutched in his trembling hands, a length of old rope rose up into the air. It turned slowly, once, and then shot forward like an arrow, coiling around the dirt-encrusted limbs of the filthy madman on the floor. They watched in silent shock as he writhed and thrashed, flopping on the tiled floor like a fish out of water as his eyes bulged and frothing spittle foamed from his lips, before falling still.

"Did you see-?" Tony's voice was barely even a whisper.

A woman emerged from out of the shadows. She was middle-aged and wearing a nurse's uniform. Her lined face was grave and concerned as she looked from the grimy body lying restrained on the floor to the pale and bloodless faces of the men before her. As she moved closer, it took Mark's mind a second to register that she must have stepped into the room through the wall itself. The air grew colder as she drew nearer, her feet making no sound on the floor and stirring up none of the debris. His torch flickered as she reached him and the hairs on his arms and the nape of his neck rose up as his skin prickled into gooseflesh.

"You should have listened," she said softly. "This place is not safe."

Tony rose to his feet and staggered for the door – his EMF meter falling to the floor as he scrabbled crazily for the handle. He disappeared out into the hallway, but Mark could hear him crashing about in the dark as he hurried blindly away.

"Go after him," she gestured, "before he hurts himself."

"But - you're what we came looking for," Mark said, his eyes widened in wonder.

"Go!" she ordered. Against the far wall the two remaining doors to the cold chambers slammed once more, and fragments of broken tile lifted from the floor and hurled themselves against the wall with savage fury, sending razor-sharp shards flying as they shattered. "Leave now!"

"But…"

"LEAVE!" she roared, the cold chamber doors slamming so hard that they buckled and the subdued patient on the floor gave a wild howl. Overhead the light fixtures flicked as though a final surge of power had been forced into them, and then exploded in a shower of glass and sparks.

Without another word Mark turned and raced after Tony, weaving his way back through the underground tunnel without so much as a backward glance.

The spirit of the nurse stood in the doorway watching him go, her arms folded. Already her body was starting to fade away as the temperature steadily rose again.

"*People,*" she smiled to herself as the single frantically-wavering torch-beam turned a corner and vanished from sight. She stepped back into the morgue, the door slamming loudly behind her as she returned to tend to her subdued patient. It was, after all, time to feed him. But first she picked up the drained EMF meter from where it had fallen and walked over to a small cabinet in the far corner. She opened it silently and placed it inside next to several other similar devices – cracked K-IIs and shattered trifield meters - and a whole collection of broken torches, lifeless EM pumps and dusty cameras. "*Why do they never listen when you're trying to help them?*"

A TOUCH OF SILENCE & OTHER TALES

The Tree By The Well

We lived in the house in a quiet corner of Wiltshire for almost a year before we discovered its terrible secret: the well and the old tree brooding next to it. That may be hard to imagine, but life was so busy that there never seemed time to properly settle and explore. My partner, Nathan, and I were renting the property, called *Heargleah*, through a private agreement with the landlord. It was a strange old house, with crooked walls and oddly angled door and window frames. Nathan, ever the joker, was quick to point out that we were not ones to worry about things being straight. Yet, with the ensuing move – entailing the steep learning curve of new jobs and getting set up in a whole new location far from family and friends – all other aspects of our lives got put on hold; including my passion for gardening.

The garden had grabbed my attention as soon as we looked at the house, so it is ironic that I neglected an exploration of it for so long. It stretched on forever; a tangled morass of vegetation, darkly tranquil, opening out beyond the spreading shade of two old oaks that stood like sentinels at the entrance. If you walked far enough into those shady depths you discovered, beyond a shallow pond surrounded by wild raspberries and hazel thickets, and hidden behind the softly swaying yellow heads of dandelion, the barest glimpse of an old crumbling wall, resting patiently within an enclosing mantle of greenery. The final fading traces of a former human presence here. Beyond this the garden turned truly feral, with spiny shrubs and coiling bramble, whilst nightshade and foxglove beguiled with poisonous beauty in the shadows cast by dense pockets of dark-berried elder.

And that, for almost a year, had been the extent of my exploration of it.

But the incessant distractions of modern life can only be obeyed for so long. Stress and the relentless demands of my job had ground me down emotionally and physically. I realised that in moving, I had lost myself along the way. All the things that brought vibrancy into my world had fallen by the wayside before the bland necessities of daily life. So I booked two weeks leave to explore the land around the house, mapping future plans for the garden, and attending to whatever things I could do right away.

I felt a rush of delight when I finally ventured beyond the broken wall. It was a glorious June morning, and the stifling heat of summer surrounded me. Pollen drifted in the air like oversized dust motes, and sunlight glinted on the cobwebs between the leaves. I was keenly aware of the sticky discomfort of my sweat-soaked t-shirt pressing against my back, but I didn't care. I had a garden to explore.

The paradox of gardens has always struck me. At first glance they can appear soothing and gentle, places to relax and soak up the sun on a summer's afternoon, or watch the golden leaves in autumn. Yet every inch is in reality a savage battleground where life and death play out constantly; a brutal struggle hidden beneath the soft green leaves and rough bark, as death feeds life.

Nature demands blood.

It has no place for mawkish sentimentality, only a ruthless drive for survival.

In some gardens this is harder to see than others. Some are so neatly manicured by the hand of humanity that the dance of life and death feels like a dirty secret hidden beneath the pruned rosebushes and tidy lawns. Others exude it proudly, wearing their wildness for all to see. This space, so long gone without anyone to tend it, was one such place. From the choking tendrils of the bind-root, to the cunning spider cocooning the fly, and the plants all desperately vying for sunlight and resources, growing against the ravenous onslaught of slug and snail; this was a garden red in tooth and thorn.

I moved through the dappled light filtering through the canopy above, surrounded by darting insects streaked with gold and scarlet. The world felt abnormally still, like time had become suspended. Carefully, I pushed aside a coiled mass of bramble heavy with ripening blackberries. My heart was racing, though I couldn't explain why. A vague sense of having stepped beyond where I was permitted had settled on me. As the thorns parted, I looked out upon a natural grassy clearing surrounded by a dense encircling boundary of ash, hawthorn and oak.

An old well of weathered grey stone lay in the heart of this clearing, beside a lone tree which was gnarled and bent with age, but whose heavy branches still bore curious fruit. Around this were the remains of a ring of toppled sarsen stones, ancient and mossy, buried beneath the tall grasses that danced and whispered in the breeze, a sound answered only by the gentle rustling of the trees bordering the clearing.

Quietly, I entered that silent circle of toppled stones, pausing to rest my hand against the closest as I passed it. I felt nothing but the smooth warm stone beneath my fingers, and for a moment laughed to myself. I'm not actually sure what I had expected to feel, but this place had an atmosphere to it, a kind of numinous reverence I had previously only felt in very old churches. For a moment I simply stood and marvelled at it all – not only the size of the clearing, but that it had remained hidden and secret for so long.

The tree was my first port of call. I stepped over a ring of toadstools that encircled it and walked slowly around the trunk, staring up at those twisted branches with fascination. It bore a deeply fissured bark and sharp thorns protruded from the branches, much like a hawthorn. However, the leaves were the wrong shape and size, and those curious fruits looked more like the spiked fruits of the deadly *datura* plant, but laced with thin veins of deep crimson.

Intrigued, I reached up to touch one, feeling the unexpected roughness of the skin. A pulsing warmth came from within it, like holding a beating heart.

I released it as sharp pain shot through my finger, and a gold and scarlet insect with iridescent wings took off into the afternoon air from the back of the fruit. I clearly saw the bone-white stinger at the tip of its abdomen. Blood had welled up like a blister on my finger, and I had an odd compulsion to wipe it on one of the leaves as I gazed up at the tree once more.

It didn't match any tree species I had seen before. I knew right away that I would need to consult my books back at the house if I had any chance of solving this enigma. So, I wandered to the well instead, gazing down into the black water which shimmered as drips fell from the moss lining the inside. The earthy fragrance filled my nose, and I took on a curious sense of tranquillity as I breathed it in, as if a great burden had lifted from my shoulders. I was aware only of the sounds of the leaves rustling around me, the gentle whispering of the grass, and the soft muted drips striking the water far below me.

I lost all track of time in the stillness of that place.

The world just fell away.

The sun was setting when I finally blinked and looked up. *Had I really been standing there all day?* It seemed impossible, but then hollow hunger growled in my stomach. I had tremors in my legs, an ache in my feet and calves.

I hurried home, knowing Nathan would have been back from work for several hours, and sure enough as I raced between the two guardian oaks towards the house, I saw both his car parked outside, and the tell-tale flicker from the television in the front room window.

"Where have you been?" he asked as I bustled in through the front door. "I've been ringing your phone for an hour."

"I was out in the garden," I said quickly. "I forgot my phone. I'm sorry."

"I was worried, Dan." He stood up, welcoming me with a hug. He was a native Wiltshire man with a quick wit and a jovial gleam in his brown eyes, not to mention a beautiful smile. I know a lot of people saw only the joker in him, but I knew that underneath lay a heart of gold and a sensitive soul. "Not like you to leave your phone behind."

"I just lost track of time," I answered. It wasn't the whole truth, but it was close enough and avoided any awkward questions that I was in no position to answer.

After dinner I left him watching a historical documentary whilst I escaped into the conservatory armed only with a Terry Pratchett book and a steaming mug of Earl Grey. Those ancient history documentaries Nathan loved were too dry for my tastes, especially ones about tombs and mummies and things buried in sand. My own guilty pleasure was re-runs of

Rosemary and Thyme, but Nathan couldn't stand it. In many ways, we were an odd couple. He loved his history and politics, and I loved music and plants. Thankfully, viewing clashes were rarely a problem because of the conservatory. It was my domain, and there, with Kate Bush blasting from the CD player, I snuggled into my favourite reading spot near the window and vanished into the Discworld.

Some time later I looked up, shivering. Dusk was falling. I sat in a tiny oasis of light cast by the lamp beside me as the growing darkness of night swallowed the room.

Setting down the book, I closed the small upper window, staring out at the sky as the liminal spell of dusk was cast over the world. The moon was rising, etching the edges of world in silvery highlights.

A small stone struck the glass next to me with such force I physically gasped. I stepped back, momentarily confused. Another hit the window directly in front of me. It glanced off and into the bushes at the side of the house. When the third stone hit the window, I snapped. Without thinking, I threw open the door and stormed out into the night, shouting angrily at whoever was doing it. But, as I furiously checked behind trees and bushes, it quickly became apparent the garden was empty.

Nathan was waiting in the doorway as I returned.

"What's going on?"

"Someone was throwing stones," I pointed at the windows. I was still shaking. "Lucky they didn't break the glass."

"Probably kids," he said, shivering. The night had stolen the heat of the day away with it.

"Or unfriendly locals," I muttered, giving the shadows one final glare. "I told you, that woman in the post office won't even look me in the eye now she knows we're not room-mates. It's like a throwback to the fifties around here."

"Can't imagine Mrs Powell hiding out here throwing stones," Nathan mused, folding his arms. "And if it was people out to cause trouble, what were you going to do to them? You hit like a wet paper bag."

"I don't know," I admitted as I stepped inside and he shut the door. "I had to do something."

I was kept awake that night by the incessant scratching of a branch against the bedroom window until it felt like my eyes would burst and my sanity might snap. Nathan never had any trouble sleeping, and I was thankful he wasn't a snorer.

My dreams when they finally came were odd, no doubt resulting from extreme fatigue. I found myself standing naked in the grass before the gnarled thorny tree, a full moon high overhead etching the branches in silver, my fingers clawing and digging into the bark. A thick sap was running from underneath it, black in the moonlight, and I leaned in, smearing my hands with it and rubbing it into my face and body, tasting its coppery taint on my tongue with a wild thrill of delight. It was only then that I realised it was blood.

I awoke late the following morning. Nathan had already gone to work, so I made toast and paced restlessly, waiting for the coffee to kick in. When I felt as close to human as I suspected I was going to get, I put on an old pair of jeans and a t-shirt, bundled several of my tree books into a rucksack and set off for the garden.

I noticed the scratches on the front door as I was locking it. There were dozens of them, covering the whole of the surface, running in lines of five. They looked like claw marks, except they were too deep and fine to have been made by a cat, and ran up the entire height of the door. Only the space around the old iron knocker was untouched. It must have happened in the night – and I felt an uneasy apprehension as I wondered if a person with a knife could have made them.

Reluctantly, I forced myself onwards into the garden. *You're being stupid*, I told myself. *Do not let this ruin your day*. But I sent a text to Nathan all the same, telling him what had happened and asking if he could get the afternoon off to help me.

I made straight for the well and the curious tree as though drawn to it. For some reason I felt safer in the hidden garden beyond the wall than I did close to the house. However, as I approached the ring of fallen sarsens I saw feathers drifting on the breeze and catching in the tall grass. Something had made a fresh kill on one of the ancient blocks. The torn carcass of a dead pigeon lay sprawled before the mid-morning sun, red splashes stark against the pale stone. This time I was sure it had been a cat. The carcass had been ripped apart. I left it alone for nature to dispose of, and hurried on to the twisted tree.

For hours I poured over my books, sitting in the shade of that tree, flicking through page after page, looking up anything that might have been the remotest match – but nothing was. As I read, I listened to the sound of the leaves rustling in the wind, and soon became aware of a different sound on the afternoon breeze: like a distant church bell or a faint wind chime. I became so entranced by it that when Nathan called out to me several hours later, I jumped.

"I sent loads of texts that I was coming home after lunch. Even tried calling," he said, as he walked into the clearing. He hadn't stopped to change, and looked hot and uncomfortable in his shirt and tie. "You weren't kidding about this place. It's impressive."

"Sorry!" I said, when a quick check of my cell phone revealed no signal at all. "No reception out here." I slipped it back into my pocket and joined him at the ring of fallen blocks.

"When you said we had a stone circle, I thought you meant a small one," he laughed. "These are almost as large as the stones in Avebury. Shame they aren't still standing."

"Druids built these, didn't they?" I frowned.

"No. Stones circles are older than that," he said, crouching down to look at the blocks. "Neolithic."

"So, not Druids?"

"Their ancestors, maybe," he shrugged. "Who knows?" He caught sight of the dead bird, still spread out in tatters across one of the larger blocks. "Behold!" he said dramatically, as he loosened his tie, "even to this day, cats still come here to sacrifice to their cat gods."

"Adorned with garlands of fresh catnip, no doubt," I smiled. He looked uncomfortable in his work clothes, dark sweat patches under his arm and down his back. "You should have changed first. You look hot."

"You look pretty good yourself," he winked, then laughed. "You sounded worried, so I came right over. I saw the door. Not sure what did that, but it looks like claw marks. Maybe a cat, or a badger?"

"World's biggest then. It goes up to the top of the door."

"Big heap of randy badgers clawing at our door?" he joked. "Look, I really don't know. But we'll keep an eye on it, and call the police if it happens again."

"That's your answer to everything," I sighed.

"That's your mystery tree?" he nodded at it. "Very *Tim Burton*. Can see why you like it."

"Still can't work out what it is, though."

"Horse chestnut, isn't it?"

"With thorns?" I gave him a wry smile. "Plus, those leaves are all wrong."

"It's a mutant horse chestnut," he smiled back. "Tell you what, I'll go and get changed, and get started on dinner. Give you a few more hours out here?"

"I'd like that. Thanks for coming home."

The afternoon sun was still warm and bright, and I felt better knowing Nathan wasn't far away, so I settled back into the shade of the tree, telling myself I would spend only one more hour at most trying to figure it out. As I flicked through the pages, feeling the texture of the paper against my fingertips, something dropped into the grass beside me, startling me out of the book. It was one of the spiked fruits.

I glanced up in surprise. The green leaves above me were now a deep golden red, curling and dropping to the ground as though in autumn, sailing down as they returned to the soil to feed the tree in death as they had in life. I scrambled to my feet in confusion, wondering what had caused this abrupt change. Those barbed branches, now devoid of leaves and fruit, looked skeletal and menacing, and I suddenly longed for the shelter of *Heargleah*.

I arrived home to find Nathan crouching by the front door putting something into an old plastic bag. He glanced around as I approached, surprised to see me.

"Finished for the day?"

I nodded. "What's that?"

"Another dead bird," he said. "Poor thing. Cats can be so evil."

"There is no evil in nature," I said, "only survival. Everything feeds on something else; a constant spiral of life out of death."

"How delightfully morbid of you. Although as a vegetarian, I don't feed on life."

"Plants are living things, dummy," I faked a laugh, but it was just a mask to cover my growing unease. I hoped Nathan wouldn't notice, but he knew me too well to be fooled.

"You feeling all right?" he asked as he tied the bag shut and dropped it into the bin.

"Still a bit spooked. First time I've felt unsafe here."

"I'll have a word with the landlord."

"That might make things worse. You're probably right, kids throwing stones and a big badger at the door."

"Let's see how things go," he said. "We've not had any trouble before. Hopefully it will all just go away again. If not, then we'll do something."

I hardly had any appetite that evening, merely picking at the lasagne that Nathan had cooked. A great weariness had come over me, and every muscle and fibre in my body ached. Nathan watched me with concern, his own plate cleaned, and when I set down my fork with a sigh he frowned.

"Is something wrong with it?"

"I'm just not hungry."

"It's your favourite."

"I'm really sorry. I'll heat it up tomorrow for lunch," I said. "I think I might be coming down with something. Feel shattered, and I ache."

"Did you drink enough today?"

"I forgot to take anything with me."

"You're probably dehydrated, it was baking out there."

"I'll take some water up to bed and get an early night."

"I'll be up later," he said, taking away my barely touched plate. "Shout if I have the TV on too loud, okay?"

The welcome stillness of the bedroom was like a soft blanket waiting to enfold me. I shut the windows despite the lingering heat of the evening and pulled the curtains closed, adding glorious darkness to the mix. The aches and weariness of the day faded from my body as I lay on the sheets and pressed my head against the pillow. I must have fallen asleep instantly, for the next thing I knew was opening my eyes to a room etched in moonlight and shadow. The curtains were drawn back and billowed in the breeze from the open windows.

My first thought was that Nathan must have opened then, but then I realised his side of the bed was empty.

"Nathan?" I called softly, turning to look at the clock.

From the foot of the bed came a sound like the scratching of thorns against wood and a shrill harsh wheeze of breath.

"Nathan?" I peered over the covers.

In the moonlight I glimpsed a hunched twisted thing crouching in the corner of the room. Spiny limbs like thorny branches tipped with slender needles, a face like old scrunched bark, and round unblinking eyes like nightshade berries. It couldn't have been more than two or three feet high.

I froze. My hands clenched into fists under the covers.

The moon passed behind a cloud, shrouding the room in darkness.

I heard the awful soft creaking of the floorboards at the side of the bed. It was coming towards me. Spiny feet scraped against wood.

I tried to scream, but the sound was locked in my throat.

My whole body was paralysed, and my eyes were useless in the blackness.

My hands were clenched so tightly I had lost all feeling in them.

The wheezing came again, from next to me now.

A sudden weight sprang up onto the bed. Then, as the clouds shifted and the moonlight returned, I stared once more into those round black eyes, inches from my own.

The scream snagged inside my throat finally burst free.

From the corner of my eye I saw the landing light come on. Nathan was rushing up the stairs.

"Dan! Dan, what's wrong?"

I blinked, and the creature was gone. Nathan was hurrying into the room.

It took him over an hour to calm me down.

He had fallen asleep in front of the television, and had woken only when he heard my cries. He had, of course, seen nothing of the creature that I had witnessed. I think he assumed it had been just a bad dream on my part.

"Do you believe in faeries?" I asked him over a mug of strong black coffee. I was sitting in the kitchen, watching the stairs carefully, in case anything came creeping down them. My hands were still trembling, and I was trying not to spill anything.

"You know I can't stand that Disney rubbish."

"I'm serious. Do you believe that there could be? Or, something, I don't know, out there that people have forgotten about? Nature spirits or…" I tailed off. I had no other explanations.

"Never really thought about it. Why? Is that what you think you saw?"

"It wasn't a bad dream," I said. "I was awake the whole time."

"Maybe it just felt that way," he suggested.

"I know the difference."

"Ok," he held up his hands. My stubbornness was legendary, and he knew when to admit defeat. "But no, I don't believe in faeries. All I know is it's gone three, and I have to go to work tomorrow."

"You better get some sleep," I said.

"Are you coming?"

I shook my head. The thought of going back into that room, even with Nathan lying next to me, was too much to bear. "I'll be up in a bit," I lied. "Just want to calm down first."

I slept downstairs on the sofa that night, with a fire poker next to me and the lights on. I hadn't actually intended to sleep, but fatigue made the choice for me. I still slept fitfully though, waking several times with a start, heart racing, certain that something would be in the room with me. I finally got up shortly before dawn, and had breakfast ready for Nathan when he came downstairs for work.

An unspoken concern hung heavily in the air as he chewed on his toast. He gave me furtive glances when he thought I wasn't looking.

"I'm all right," I assured him finally, pouring a fresh cup of coffee for both of us.

"You haven't been yourself lately," he said softly. "These panic attacks, and this talk about faeries? Maybe you should go and see the doctor? I know how stressed you've been at work. There's no shame in needing help with that."

"I'm not depressed, or having a breakdown," I assured him. "I just... I'm fine, really."

"Text or call, if you need anything," he said. "I'm in a meeting most of the morning, but around this afternoon."

"Thanks, but don't worry," I said, reaching over to straighten his tie.

He touched my hand. "I'm here for you. Let me help."

"You do," I answered, brushing my finger against his cheek.

After he had gone, I spent the morning pottering about the house. The garden no longer called to me like it had previously, and in truth, I knew I was avoiding it. Everything had started the moment I found that clearing and the tree. I knew it somehow. It was irrational, it made no sense, but it felt like I had woken something by going there – or at least, drawn its attention. I remembered the blood I had been compelled to wipe onto its leaves, and shivered.

I tried to tell myself I was being crazy, reading too much into things. Now in the cold light of day some perverse part of my being had even started to question if I had simply dreamed or imagined the creature in the corner of the room. I no longer knew what to trust or what to think. I only hoped that perhaps if I stayed away, whatever was happening might do the same.

I had just finished sorting through the bathroom cupboards around eleven, when a crash thundered downstairs, followed by the sound of something rolling across the kitchen floor. With my heart in my throat I hurried downstairs, grabbing a spray bottle of bathroom bleach which I brandished like a gun. It wasn't much of a weapon, but it felt better to have something.

The kitchen cupboards were all open and glass jars and tins were rolling across the floor as I edged into the room. The cereal boxes were also on their side, and a whole bag of flour had been emptied over the kitchen table.

Anger and fear surged within me at the same time, like water bursting from a geyser. "Get out of our house!" I shouted furiously, whirling around the room, checking corners and peering under the table for any sign of an intruder. But aside from all the mess, nothing else looked out of place in any other room, and all the doors were still locked. I felt hopelessly vulnerable, knowing that these things could come into my home at any time, and knowing that Nathan didn't believe me.

Reluctantly, I made an effort to tidy the kitchen, but my skin was still crawling and I kept glancing over my shoulder, convinced I was being watched. The whole house felt different, changed somehow. I saw something jutting out from underneath one of the old heavy cupboards. It was the edge of an old photograph, covered in years of dust and lint. I pulled it free and carefully wiped it clean over at the sink. As I cleared away the layers of accumulated grime, I realised it was of the stone circle and the strange tree that grew within it. Half of the stones were still standing in it, but the rest looked as overgrown and wild as it did today, and the tree was unchanged, still as gnarled and twisted as I knew it, and still clearly bearing those curious spiny fruits. Spidery handwriting covered the back of the image in ink that had faded with the years, but was just still legible: "*Abandoned ring of stones around the cursed 'Unseelie tree' 1934*".

Unseelie. The word rang a bell somewhere in my memory, and I frantically tried to recall where I had seen or heard it before. Drawing a blank, I snatched up my phone to run a search on the word, when I noticed a missed call was showing in the top corner of the display, along with the icon that I had an unplayed message waiting.

It was from Nathan.

"I got your text," he said, sounding anxious. "What's happened? I'll be home as early as I can, but I can't keep doing this. I think the boss is about ready to lynch me."

A cold chill ran through me as I dialled his number. I hadn't sent him a text. I hadn't touched my phone all day until now. But there was no answer, and suddenly as I stood there, I realised I could also hear his phone ringing from outside the window too.

Nathan's car was parked in the driveway. The doors were all open, and the paintwork was covered in hundreds of deep scratches. The phone still rang from inside Nathan's jacket folded on the seat, but there was no sign of him. My heart quickened and the first flutters of panic stirred as I noticed the churned gravel by the driver's side door. It looked like something had been struggling or dragged across the driveway and towards those two oaks in the garden.

I ran to the sarsen stones in a blind panic. My head swimming as uneasy thoughts and fears struck me like storm waves against a rock. Something ahead was blowing in the breeze, like large pieces of black, white and blue confetti. I realised a moment later it was the remains of Nathan's clothes, torn to ragged shreds. His watch lay on one of the sarsens, smashed and gleaming in the sunlight, and I tripped over one of his shoes in the long grass as I hurried towards the tree by the well.

There was something in the tree, but I couldn't make out what it was at first because the sun was directly in my eyes. But as I drew closer, my worst fears became real.

It was Nathan.

He hung naked and upside down from those thorny branches. His body riddled with deep scratches and lacerations, as if he had been pulled through a mass of thorns. His throat had been ripped open, and his glassy eyes stared sightlessly at me from a red mask of dried blood.

My knees gave out and I collapsed onto the grass.

I didn't cry or scream. I just stared, my whole body shaking. Some part of my mind battled against my senses, telling me that this *couldn't* be real.

Meadowsweet, lavender and heather had been bound into his hair and also around his pubic region, and strands of greenery had been carefully wound around his penis like some kind of bizarre maypole.

The blood had long since stopped flowing, and what remained around the wounds was coagulated, buzzing with flies. But his blood had sprayed out across the grass, soaking into the dark soil around the roots of the tree as though nourishing it.

That was when I screamed. It was a wail of anguish that I didn't think would end. I screamed until my lungs ached and it seemed my heart would burst from the effort, as my hands clawed into the soil as though trying to get back all the blood that had drained into it.

It was the feeling of being watched that finally spurred me to my senses. The rustling leaves whispered and taunted, and I had to get away from the awful sight in that tree. I couldn't bring myself to try moving his body, so I fled back to the house.

The feeling of being watched followed me all the way home.

I never called the police. There's nothing they can do, and I know they'd never find the body even if they looked. Why drag others into this? Instead, I am sitting now, writing these words for you. I don't know if *they* will let you find them, and I no longer care.

Soon I'll hear those little hands rattling at the windows, the sharp claws scraping against the door. They'll come for me, because they have long been without offerings, and are hungry for blood now that I have drawn their attention to us.

I won't run. Without Nathan, there is nowhere I want to go.

At least this way, I might be with him again soon.

Our ancient ancestors recognised the raw power of nature. They built stone circles to honour and chart it, and made offerings in efforts to placate it. They understood what we have since forgotten, that nature is the true master of this world, not humanity; and, that it is often terrifying and brutal. The death of one life is but a harvest for the next.

We have lost our place in the natural order. We cloak our wildness behind designer labels, social conventions and fancy new technologies, but it is all still there, lurking raw and primal just beneath the surface. All the denial in the world won't change that.

For all our advances and discoveries, a simple and single truth remains.

The blood feeds the land, as it always has.

Natural Selection

For Jane McCaa

The beetles were feeding again. Breaking and crushing loose chunks of rock with their sharp mandibles and extracting the metal ores within; digesting them to reinforce their own metallic brown elytra that glinted with a dull lustre in the late afternoon sunlight.

Nearby, crouching on the edge of a low grassy ridge, micro-definition camera clutched excitedly in her hands, Rebecca Aaron watched these unique creatures in rapt fascination, even though she had seen them feed countless times before. She lifted the small recorder to her bulky breather unit, dictating into it between snaps of the camera, knowing that the beetles wouldn't react to her presence.

"The native coleoptera are the largest of their kind I have ever seen," she noted. "Their adult size is roughly equivalent to that of a small dog; measuring on average between fourteen to eighteen inches in length, and eight to ten inches in width. Their larvae are each at least the size of a mouse. Like the beetles back on Earth, they have the characteristic sheath-like elytra and complex chewing mouthparts; and their larvae are sedentary blind grubs, with the typical three pairs of legs on the thorax."

Clicking off the recorder she edged forward, spellbound as these huge but harmless giants wandered around their nest site - something more common for ants than beetles; yet these coleoptera showed all signs of an intricately developed social structure. But that was only part of the appeal of these incredible insects - there was so much about them that was unique and unknown, so much still to document and understand of their complex biology. She couldn't deny it, she was hooked.

Shifting closer and lying flat against the damp terracotta soil, she angled her camera at the closest insect, trying to capture as many varied images as she could get, hoping for some insight into their behaviour that had so far eluded her. One of the smaller beetles, clearly a juvenile, lumbered over to her, exploring. She flattened her hand, allowing the beetle to roam across it, the bristly legs tickling and probing her skin. Its powerful mandibles flexed and clicked, but Rebecca wasn't concerned. She'd quickly learned in her months of study that they were absolutely harmless, despite their fearsome appearance and incredible strength; she could even walk barefoot amongst them in safety. Metal ore was the only thing that interested them, and while she didn't yet understand how they managed to draw sustenance from it, she had discovered that they ignored processed metals and alloys altogether.

It still astounded her that the prospectors and settlement scouts who had visited this world back in the thirties had deemed it valueless, just another rock not worth the effort of terraforming. That decision had been made mainly because the ores and minerals it contained were of no use for industrial purposes. The fact that the air was slightly toxic and required the use of filtering masks to breathe had also played a major part in discouraging settlers from coming here.

So much the better, for Rebecca had no love for the human race.

Although her life and career as a zoologist derived from her deep passion for studying the myriad forms of life that were constantly being discovered on newly charted worlds, coleoptera and arachnids especially, her heart remained cold toward her own species; noisy, destructive and self-centered humanity, moving and spreading like a cancer through the stars. It angered her to think that after having torn up, squandered and abused the Earth's precious natural resources, they had now widened the process to the other planets in the universe. It also enraged her that the prospectors who had found this world, and the scientists who had traveled with them, had assessed the indigenous giant beetle population as worthless and unremarkable. To her, although they were clearly creatures of limited intelligence, they were far more intriguing than most people she had known, not to mention preferable company - never talking too much, never criticizing, never breaking promises or letting her down. With her beetles it was a straightforward case of 'what you saw was what you got', pure and simple. And what she saw was as close to a slice of heaven as she had ever experienced in this cold, godless universe.

That was when she'd arranged to come out here. She'd been surprised with the speed at which her research grant had been cleared, having expected the usual tiresome delays at the dithering hands of bureaucracy who reveled in gift-wrapping all requests in red tape. She suspected it had something to do with the fact that her colleagues at the Zoological Institute had never gotten along with her. Deep down, even Rebecca had to admit that with her single-minded drive and burning obsession to achieve results at the exclusion of all else, she wasn't the easiest of people to get along with. She had managed to put more than a few noses out of joint along the way. Her colleagues themselves – a group for whom she had little time and even less respect, had called her a bitter and jaded cynic, incapable of warmth and compassion. Some had even remarked – when they thought she was out of earshot - how sorry they felt for the beetles, having to put up with her.

Rebecca honestly didn't care what they thought. After all, Dian Fossey hadn't been truly appreciated in her own time either. The best people never were.

It was getting late now. Growing shadows crept across the land, as the sun set in the blood-red sky. Reluctantly, Rebecca slipped her camera into its case and set off through the dense brown vegetation that covered the planet; picking her way through glistening leaves and vines slick with moisture, surrounded by small clustered clouds of buzzing insects, the earthy-smelling mulch squishing damply underfoot. The humid, sticky air made her tee-shirt clammy against her skin, and sweat darkened the areas under her armpits and down her back, but she barely noticed, having long grown used to such discomforts.

The planet itself had no official name - just a basic seven digit coordinate code, but she had taken it upon herself to name her new home. She had chosen Karisoke, in honour of the study site where Dian Fossey had worked for twenty-two years studying mountain gorillas. For although Fossey had lived and died long before Rebecca had been born, her work, life and sheer dedication to her chosen field had been a major source of inspiration.

Halfway to the habitation module Rebecca stopped, looking out over a small gorge at the lush tropical plant-life and massive savannas of Karisoke, hearing the cries, calls and hooting wails of the animals forming the planet's complex ecosystem. Somewhere deep in the vegetation, something ponderous picked its way along, its clumsy progress sending flocks of wild flying creatures winging into the sky with angry, startled shrieks. The setting sun cast a glossy reddish sheen across the foliage, making it look as though the leaves and grass were awash with blood. Large floating seeds and spores drifted lazily in the air like oversized dust motes. The tropical beauty and solitude of this world never failed to strike her with awe. It was a place full of wild, dramatic splendour; but the savage efficiency of the natural world had always appealed to her. Little was wasted here, everything had a purpose and a reason for being - a link in the great and fragile ecosystem. It had taken her a while to get used to the sight of brown vegetation, so different from the chlorophyll green that populated her own world. But then, so much here had taken time to grow accustomed to at first. The sky was always a deep orange-red during the day, turning a dark and moody purple-black when it rained. The night was much darker than on Earth, with no cities to cast light pollution. There was also no moon to reflect the light from the system's sun after dark, leading to some of the darkest nights she had ever seen - but allowing the stars in all their beauty to shine through; not that she could pick out any familiar constellations from here, although they were all still out there: Orion, Taurus, Canis Major, The Big Dipper. She was just seeing them from the wrong angle to make them out.

Yes, this stunning world was hers alone, as were the beetles, and it was a great joy to her not to have to share it. Nor was that likely ever to change, since most people tended to cluster on the nearest habitable planets closest to Earth. For despite the way it had been popularly fictionalized before commercial space travel became a reality, the truth had quickly hit home to the people of the Earth: space was a big disappointment. Interstellar travel was long and tedious, lacking amenities and comfort. The under-supplied colonies were cramped, difficult to maintain, and often rife with crime and racial hostility. Space had also opened up hitherto unknown diseases and viral pathogens, and had found new dangerous animals that made the scorpions, rattlesnakes and black widows of Earth look harmless by comparison. Yes, the novelty had quickly faded, and few were curious enough to brave the discomforts to travel beyond the overcrowded colony worlds.

Arriving back at her battered habitation module, she let herself inside the inner-lock, and purged the outside atmosphere before removing her breather and stepping into the artificially purified and filtered environment. Overhead fans turned lazily, beating back the stifling humidity.

She pulled the clasp from her dark hair, and ran a hand through it, shaking it down around her shoulders. Kicking off her boots, she switched on the light and powered up her computer terminal, ready to record the day's findings and store them onto a DHT chip. As she slipped in a spare chip and keyed in her observations for the day, she glanced up with a smile at the small web in the corner of the room.

Incy was out and about.

She stood, stretching wearily, one hand lazily brushing an errant strand of hair back behind her ear; then leaned over, peering closely at him. He was truly a handsome specimen, even for a common house spider. Eight long, slender legs delicately balanced on the web, avoiding the sticky snare-lines; pedipalps carefully feeling and sensing the world around it. Like coleoptera, arachnids never ceased to amaze and impress her. Unlike the stumbling progress of humanity who took years to develop, grow and learn as they limped clumsily toward adulthood, spiders were born with the knowledge of how to spin webs and hunt. They were survivors, and had followed humanity - first as they explored the planet Earth, settling even into arctic research stations and remote settlements - and then, finally, on the giant leap into space. Incy, as she had named him, must have traveled with her inside one of the storage crates, for there were no natural arachnids on Karisoke.

"How's your day been?" She asked jokingly, taking care not to disturb the web as she spoke. It seemed unlikely that the sealed and filtered air supply of the habitat would provide an opportunity for any flies or tropical mosquitoes to get inside the living space to feed Incy. But sometimes they did manage to get in - possibly through the airlock with her when she returned home each day. Sometimes she would catch some for him, and release them near his web, so that they flew in as they escaped the confines of her container.

Outside there came the first faint rumbles of thunder, and large dime-sized drops of rain began to slap against the roof of the habitat. Rebecca turned the switch on the lamp units, brightening the crowded interior, as the rain lashed down upon the world outside in unbroken sheets of water. The steady *hissing* spray drowning out all other sounds, drumming on the roof and windows, forming a constant background sound, as she finished her reports of the day's observations and reviewed briefly the notes she had taken on her tenth day, when she had caught and dissected one of the beetles - a task she had painfully regretted, but one which had been invaluable in providing some clues to the remarkable life-cycle and digestive process of these remarkable insects.

Finally she sat back in her chair with an exhausted sigh, rubbing her eyes with her fingers, feeling the first tell-tale signs of a headache starting there. She pushed back the chair and stood, stretching and arching her aching back, making slow lazy circles of her head and hearing her neck click as she did. It had been a long day, tiring but rewarding. Despite the weariness that settled upon her, she felt alive and connected to the planet around her, a sense of home and belonging that she had never experienced on Earth. Hard to believe she had only been out here two months now. Sometimes it was as though she had always known this place. As if the planet Earth had been nothing but a crazy, chaotic dream of noise, pollution and heaving masses of ignorant and annoying human beings.

Outside the rain continued to *hiss* against the habitat, a continuous and unceasing white noise that some might have found irritating, but that she merely found soothing. If it hadn't been for the toxic air outside, she might have peeled off her sweat-stained tee-shirt and muddy khaki pants and simply walked outside, enjoying the coolness of the air and water as it washed the accumulated grime and sweat from her skin. Instead, she would settle for a regular shower in the tiny, cramped cubical that was barely large enough for her to squeeze into.

Nights were quiet here on Karisoke, away from the rush and bustle of colonised worlds; although they were never fully silent, filled as they were with the furtive rustling, hooting and bellowing of life in all its myriad forms, getting about the business of living, hunting and self-perpetuation. But while others might have found the isolation and lack of a social nightlife distressing and even maddening, Rebecca welcomed it with open arms. Had it been a physical, tangible thing she might very well have wrapped herself in it like a thick, warm blanket. She had no need for human companionship, out here she was free and the world was hers to savour and enjoy. The breather spoilt the illusion a little, but the magic of the atmosphere was unsullied. She still recalled vividly the first night, when Karisoke had welcomed her with a spectacular meteor shower, that lit the night sky like a hundred blazing streamers of fire as the meteors burned up in the lower ionosphere, victims of air friction. Although she had not seen anything quite like that since, each night never failed to offer her something new and wonderful - from the sunsets that simply dazzled her with their overwhelming beauty, to the nocturnal mating of some kind of native fireflies.

Tonight however, it seemed the regularly scheduled show had been cancelled, due to rain.

That night she had trouble dropping off to sleep, the headache had hit with full force, suddenly and sadistically transforming itself from a nagging ache into a full-blown skull cracking migraine. The paracetamol patch she had administered had done nothing for it.

She finally fell asleep in the still hours shortly after midnight, when the rain had petered off to a fine drizzle. The last sound she heard was the trickling of water from the roof of the habitat, and her dreams were filled with vivid memories of the river by the house on Earth, where she had lived as a child.

*

The next morning, she knew as she opened her eyes that her simple headache of the night before had been nothing less than the vanguard of a full blown virus. Her whole body was chilled to the core, and her head throbbed madly, the pain seemingly centered behind her aching eyes. At least there was no sign of the usual sore throat that normally always accompanied such things, and that left her feeling as if each swallow contained broken glass and sandpaper. She rolled weakly onto her side, drawing back the blind and peering out, her sensitive eyes flinching at the intense brightness of the light. The rain had completely stopped, and the ground and vegetation sparkled with a reddish sheen in the sunlight.

A suddenly dizziness overcame her as she swung her legs out of the bed and stood up, and she sat heavily back down. She rested for a few minutes with her head in her hands, hair flowing down over her fingers, as she waited for the sensation to pass. She had drugs and medicines aplenty in her supply case, so finding something to ease the discomfort wouldn't be hard, but it was damn inconvenient when she had been looking forward to a full day in the field with her beetles.

She slipped on a fresh tee-shirt and then grabbed her thick jacket - something she had brought with her, but never yet needed on this tropical planet. She was still intensely cold, and walked slowly to a mirror. Her own face, ghostly pale and shivering, framed with her disheveled morning hair stared back at her. *God, I look terrible*, she thought. Suddenly an intense shiver raced through her and she grabbed the edge of the counter as the habitat spun and churned around her. She squeezed her eyes shut, then stumbled desperately toward the small enclosed bathroom as the intense urge to vomit welled up within her. She barely made it in time, and after the distasteful deed was done, she sat on the floor with her arms wrapped around her, shivering. Perhaps today would be better spent indoors after all, she decided.

Three hours later, after taking some of the high-strength Permaxical from her medicine cabinet, she felt a little more in control of herself. The shivering had subsided as had the nausea, although the damn headache stubbornly refused to leave and pulsed like an evil heart beating right behind her eyes. She spent the next hour staring out the window, at the clouds drifting lazily overhead, and watching the arboreal creatures soar and wing above and around the tree line. Finally she decided enough was enough - she felt better now; not a hundred per cent, no - but certainly up for a visit to her beetles, although she would give her usual morning jog a miss. Besides, it was maddening to be stuck inside the habitat, even if she did have Incy for company. The filtered air in here always seemed stale, as though something wholesome had been removed during the purification process, and she had never been much of an indoor person anyway.

Rebecca actually began to feel a little better as she trudged slowly along the path she had marked, back toward the beetles' nest. The breather unit seemed a little heavier today, her steps were slower and lacked her usual enthusiasm, and her limbs were like clumsy lead weights - but it was good to be outside and roaming freely.

She gazed out across the gorge as she passed it, a habit that she had developed since her first day, for the view was always breathtaking. Today a low ground mist covered the area, adding a mysterious, hazy quality to the landscape as it swirled. Above this came the screeching chorus of the arboreal creatures, interspersed with the rustling and grunts of other animals hunting and feeding in the tall ferns between the trees. She waited there for a few minutes, her breathing calmer and her head, despite feeling like her sinuses were stuffed with warm cotton wool, felt a little more focused. Then she continued, as fast as her uncooperative limbs would allow, on toward the nest site.

She settled down on her favourite rock overlooking the nest. As she had expected for this time of the day, the nest was a hive of bustling activity – but she quickly noticed some kind of commotion among a small group of the beetles not too far from where she was sitting. Standing clumsily and almost overbalancing, Rebecca crept closer, wishing her head didn't feel like it was spinning quite as much. A group of about ten to fifteen coleoptera had surrounded a single member of the group, who was standing over the torn carcass of a juvenile. Judging by the dark blood staining the mandibles of the larger insect, it had been responsible for the death of the younger one. Rebecca watched with captivated interest. During her observations she had witnessed a few fights - possibly struggles to assert dominance or leadership, but had never witnessed one of the beetles actually kill another before.

What happened next took her completely by surprise.

With a speed, coordination and ferocity that startled her, the surrounding beetles charged toward the singled out individual, the light glinting from their metallic chitinous forewings as they converged and tore into the victim, stripping away its shiny brown elytra in a ruthless attack. Then, as quickly as it had started, it was all over, and the beetles all withdrew as one. Rebecca edged closer still, putting one hand out against a nearby rock to steady herself, caution giving way to curiosity as she leaned forward to get a better look. To her astonishment the singled-out beetle was still alive, but its hard protective casing had been totally removed, and the remaining coleoptera were now gently herding it towards the edge of the nest site, while yet more gently carried away the remains of the slain juvenile.

Excitement fluttered in Rebecca as she watched the proceedings. This had never been expected, not behaviour of this kind. Had she just seen what she thought she had seen? Had they just punished one of their members for murdering another? By removing his protective shell, they had in essence left him defenseless to the elements - and now they were clearly casting him out of the nest site.

Just wait, she smiled to herself, momentarily forgetting her own physical discomfort. *When those idiots at the institute read about this, they're going to be kicking themselves.* But suddenly that same thought chilled her, and the smile slipped from her face. If she told them, they'd want to send more people out here to assist her. *I think I'll hold off on submitting this, at least until I make some more observations. And that*, she thought smugly, *could take months.*

By the time she got home dusk had settled on the land, and she collapsed onto her bed, totally exhausted. She curled onto her side, not even bothering to get undressed, and fell into a deep and delicious sleep.

In her dreams she was back on Earth, heading into the imposing glass and steel headquarters of the Zoological Institute to hear the final decision regarding her request to transfer to Karisoke to study the indigenous beetle population there.

She stepped inside and carefully removed her breather unit, and the protective membranes from her eyes, storing them in the container of cleaning solution she always carried with her. The pollution levels of the Earth had grown to such an extent that such measures were required. She moved briskly down the hallway from the stark metal reception area, past rooms where biologists and scientists were busily scurrying about in their white lab coats, like frantic mice locked within a maze too vast and insidious for them to see or comprehend. Within minutes she was being admitted into the main meeting area on the administration level, an ugly room of stark modern efficiency; gleaming glass, chrome and steel, dark varnished woods and shiny marbled flooring. An artificial kingdom ruled by flawed and blind people. Self-elected gods in a shrine of plastic and polymers, ruling their judgments over the natural world they had secretly forsaken.

This is it, she told herself bitterly. *They're going to deny my request. They know how much I want this, so they'll keep me from it.* She knew they disliked her - said she was too outspoken; accused her of clinging to ideas and beliefs not suited to the modern age. She had no time for their opinions, and no desire to listen to their pompous debating - but the truth was, if she had any hope of getting to Karisoke, she needed their approval.

That had been the day they had all surprised her, and allowed her to go...

*

When she awoke the next morning, it was to an agony which made the previous day's illness seem like a dress rehearsal. It was a little before dawn when she opened her eyes, aware that her whole body was shivering - despite the fact that she was drenched in sweat. She threw the damp, wrinkled sheets aside, and staggered to her feet - almost falling to the floor as another wave of dizziness swept over her. Each breath she took was like inhaling a lung-full of burning acid, and her clammy skin looked horribly yellowed with the clear signs of jaundice.

No way is this just a simple viral infection, she thought, slumping down into her chair before her computer terminal. She reached over and grabbed the front of the medicine cabinet, thankful it was well stocked to last until the next supply vessel arrived to bring her fresh equipment. She applied three Taslodex patches to her arms, slightly more than the recommended average dose, but she was far from caring about that, and slumped back with her eyes closed. As she rested, she tried to figure out what might be causing this sudden illness. However, as far as she could recall she had neither been bitten or stung by any of the flora or fauna here, nor had she been outside without a breather unit. Her fruits and vegetables were grown inside a separate hydroponics unit attached directly to her habitant, and the air and water running into them were filtered and purified. Surely there was something she was missing, but what? The beetles? No, that was unlikely, she'd studied them closely for two months now, and there was nothing harmful about them, they certainly contained no toxins...

She opened her eyes an hour later and realized she had fallen asleep in the chair. Her neck was stiff, her aching body wracked with shivers, and her damp clothes were pasted to her clammy skin with sweat.

She climbed gingerly to her feet, intending to take some Permaxical to augment the Taslodex patches she had applied earlier, before slipping into bed. However, she froze with her hand resting on the medicine cabinet, staring into the corner of the habitat.

Incy lay curled in a tight ball on the surface of the desk just below his web.

She didn't have to touch him to know he was dead, and at sight of him a dreadful suspicion crept into her mind. Walking stiffly and slowly, she passed along the small sectional corridor leading into the hydroponics bay and opened the door. When the door slid aside she stared in numb shock, her worst suspicions becoming a cruel reality before her eyes.

The plants in the bay, transported as seeds from Earth, were turning brown and wilting. Their leaves were starting to shrivel, horribly imitating the way Incy had curled in death.

There was no doubt now. There was a breach somewhere in the habitat and toxic air from outside was steadily leaching in.

She hurried back into the habitat, stumbling against the desk as her legs gave way beneath her. The urge to defecate suddenly came upon her, a sensation like a small tornado was churning within her bowels, and she barely had time to scrabble her way into the small bathroom before a stinging stream of waste came pouring from within her.

When she at last emerged from the bathroom, pale and shivering, her vision starting to blur and her stomach feeling no less stable than it had a few moments before, the first thing she did was reach for the breather. It was the only thing she could do. Maybe once she stopped breathing the unfiltered air, the side-effects of her exposure to the toxic atmosphere would pass. Then she could set about finding and sealing the leak into the habitat.

But as her fingers closed around the breather, it crumbled in her grip, breaking into several brittle plastic and metal fragments that clattered to the floor. Puzzled, she grabbed the spare breather lying beside it - but again, the same thing happened. At the sight of this the despair and the miserable agony became unbearable and she sank to her knees, sobbing in bitter frustration.

It's not fair! Why the hell is this happening! She drove her fist down onto the desk, pounding the surface until the rage within subsided, trying not to give in to the terror that followed in its wake.

Something scuttled quickly across the floor, catching her attention, and she looked up in time to see it scurry beneath her bed.

Rebecca watched it with confused and mesmerized horror, convinced for a moment that she must have been seeing things. Then it hit her. It had been one of the coleoptera that she had been studying - but what had it been doing so far from the nest? She had never seen any come this far before.

A quick relocation of her bed revealed a large opening in the habitat wall, the edges of which had clearly been torn open by the sharp mandibles of the beetles - yet the metal, being processed from various alloys, had simply been discarded on the ground and not consumed.

Why would they...?

Then another terrible thought hit her, and she hurried outside, staggering and almost bent double as a sharp cramp cut through her. Her bowels opened again before she could stop herself, and she collapsed onto the dark soil, tears blurring her eyes.

When she finally made it around the other side of the habitat, she opened the protective panel covering the air filter system, and peered inside. The whole unit had been shredded and torn apart, the twisted fragments littered the floor of the compartment - and in the far wall was another hole, again large enough for the beetles to squeeze in through.

It was then that the true state of things came slamming home like a sledgehammer blow. With no breathers, no air filter - and not enough spare parts to completely rebuild the damaged unit, there was no chance at all to survive. The next supply vessel wasn't due for months, and the Zoological Institute wouldn't grow suspicious when she didn't report in, because Rebecca had a noted habit of going for long periods without contacting them.

For a long time Rebecca simply knelt there, staring at the ruin that had once been her life-line. She had been advised not to come by the institute, or at least to come with a team, but she had refused; her own antisocial preferences winning out over common sense. She had refused the extra equipment they said she needed. She wanted to show them she didn't need them or their ways. And now this had come of it.

She raised a trembling hand to her mouth, her body and senses suddenly numb and cold. The world around her was suddenly too bright - too starkly defined and in colours that seemed unreal and garish. The world swayed like the deck of a boat on a stormy ocean, but she squeezed her eyes tight and fought against the urge...*the need*...to vomit.

The desperate scream that had been building within her all this time now broke free; a hoarse, ragged scream of terrified, hopeless, misery. The disbelief and a sense of sudden loneliness, unlike any she had felt before, overwhelmed her like a foul and stinking cloud of fetid darkness; sapping her spirit and threatening to send her mind and sanity tumbling into a churning helter-skelter of senseless chaos.

For now there was nowhere to go, and nothing to be done.

*

When the supply ship arrived two months later, there was no sign of the habitat in the clearing. Only a few remaining fragments of twisted metal remained, sticking up out of the ground like the bones of some long dead corpse. Only after digging and poking around the underbrush did the rest of the habitat turn up - in fragments scattered throughout the bushes and buried beneath the damp terracotta soil.

Rebecca Aaron's body was found shortly afterward, not far from the clearing, badly decomposed and heavily picked over by animals to the point of being virtually unrecognizable. In the curled claw of bone and rotting flesh that once had been her hand, they found a single battered DHT chip, badly corroded by the elements and caked with dirt. Much of the chip was corrupted beyond repair, except for the last handful of entries - mostly observations from her last few days of study. But along with them, the members of the Zoological Institute also found her final message when, her body slowly dying from the poisonous atmosphere against which she now had no protection, she had fought against her sickness to record her own fate:

"It's getting cold. The roof is leaking, and the floor's flooded. It's hard to keep writing - fingers are trembling so bad I keep missing the keys. There's a burning in my stomach now. It's getting hard to breathe, too.

The beetles are outside. I can see them in the fading light. Jesus, they're just *waiting* out there, not even moving. There must be hundreds of them - looks like the whole damn lot of them. At least, all the ones from the nest I was studying anyway. I think they're watching me. I think they know what they've done...stripped away my protection, leaving me vulnerable...just like that outcast beetle that I saw. Sounds crazy, but that's what they're doing. Did I once say I thought them unintelligent? What the hell was I thinking? What was I seeing - what was there, or what I wanted to? I can't believe I never saw that in their nature, their complex social order, so unlike the normal behaviour of coleoptera. God, I was so stupid!

...They started attacking the habitat today, tearing into it with those mandibles of theirs, ripping chunks out of it like it was paper! I crawled out, and they let me go - right through them. Those little bastards even cleared a space for me. I tried to get a few of them as I went...but they're too fast for me. My whole body is burning up. I think my eyesight's going. Everything is so blurry now.

I can't keep writing. Fingers can't find the keys too well at all now. Power cell in the portable terminal is fading. I'll save what I can to DHT. I hope they don't break that apart too. It's so cold here. I think I'm just going to sleep for a while now. Just a little while.

One last thought keeps running through my head though. It should be funny, but it's not. I keep thinking how my colleagues wanted to see the back of me, and how they pitied the beetles for having to put up with me.

Jesus, where did it all go wrong?"

Sidhe Brook

There had always been stories about Sidhe Brook for as long as I could remember - sinister tales of travellers who had gone missing there on misty nights, and of local children who had vanished whilst playing near the stream before dusk on midsummer's eve or on the winter solstice.

The brook itself was a place of unusual natural beauty — secluded and wonderfully peaceful, surrounded by hills covered in vibrant growths of wildflowers and crested with ancient trees of oak, ash and hawthorn. From the tall grasses beside the narrow road and by the old bridge there grew clusters of lily of the valley, lavender, thyme and foxglove, and thick red and white fly agaric toadstools grew fat and numerous amongst the fallen and rotting trunks of the oldest trees. Still more of these poisonous speckled mushrooms grew in a wide and irregular circle on a grassy hillock not far from the road and the bridge, close to a lone hawthorn whose trunk was oddly gnarled and twisted.

It was a place of unearthly stillness, where even the soft gurgling of the brook faded away if you sat for long enough next to it, and a lingering sense of otherworldly magic hung in the air at all times of the year, even when the barren grip of winter held the land in its icy embrace.

All of us had, at one time or another, heard the faint sounds of music drifting into the village from the direction of the brook on the evening breeze; usually on nights when the full moon sat high in the sky, or at twilight on the solstices. People rarely spoke openly of it, and would hurry quickly inside on such nights, locking doors and securing windows, whilst mothers checked urgently on their children – for it was widely believed that anyone who stood and listened to that faint but haunting melody for too long would soon fall under its spell and be drawn away into the night, never again to be seen in this land.

"The Fae Folk dance on those hills and play in that brook," my mother had warned me darkly when I had been a child and old enough to understand, and I had known from the look in her hazel eyes that she had been deathly serious. "And you'd best not be there to see them when they do, or you'll never come home again."

Whenever I would ask to go out to play, she would always insist that I carry an old iron nail in each pocket, or else she would tie a small bag of dried herbs to my belt, telling me to avoid the brook at noon and dusk and to never go there alone. But I always did. I remember on many occasions I would creep through the morning grass still damp with dew, and crouch expectantly behind a bush or tree, watching and waiting patiently for a glimpse of the Fae. Most of the time there was nothing, and I would trudge home feeling disappointed and empty. But there was one time when I had been out playing in the glorious April sunshine and, on a whim, had set off into the dense woodlands. I loved playing in those overgrown depths. A sense of deep mystery and tranquillity always surrounded me there. I moved between ancient trees whose bloated and lichen-covered trunks had stood for eternity, and picked my way through twisted coils of brambles, around clusters of nettles and past a dense blackthorn, now bright and beautiful with white blossom that treacherously hid the long thorns. The sunlight dappled the forest floor and birdsong and furtive rustlings filled the air around me, but gradually it seemed that the deeper I moved into that green oasis of life the more subdued the birdsong became and the louder those furtive rustlings grew. I knew this forest would lead me out near Sidhe Brook, and I realized also I was half holding my breath with anticipation, hoping to catch sight of the Fae. I slipped silently from the tree line, my trousers covered in green burs, and settled down behind one of the old oaks overlooking the brook and the hawthorn near its faerie ring. The sun was warm enough to take the lingering chill out of the spring breeze, and soon my eyes became heavy. I resolved to stay awake, but my willpower proved inadequate to the task, and I awoke to find nightfall creeping upon the land. My initial annoyance was quickly curbed when I realised that I could hear the sound of bells and a gentle and haunting melody floating through the dusk air.

I recognised it at once from the strange and distant sounds we had all heard at night from time to time – music that the adults had warned us was the song of the Fae.

With my heart racing and my throat dry, I sat up and knelt to peer around the trunk of the tree against which I had been resting. For a moment I thought I could hear the sound of voices and laughter amongst the music. I held my breath as I leaned further out – but as I moved one of the old nails fell from my pocket. I quickly tried to grab it, but my clumsy lunge only managed to hit it further down the slope.

In that instant the music stopped abruptly, and I glanced up in time to see a vague flurry of motion near the tree line. It was so fast I barely had time to register it, but a mix of panic and elation ran through me like a wave. I was frozen to the spot - my eyes transfixed on the growing shadows between the trees and my heart was pounding like a furious drum, seemingly in the back of my throat. I couldn't even breathe for fear of making a sound.

It was several minutes before I could move again, but it felt like hours. Gradually I edged forward, my eyes never leaving the tree line, and my groping hand quickly recovered the nail from the grass and slipped it back into my pocket.

The woods were still and silent now, but I knew two things with absolute surety: the first was that I had not imagined it, and the second was that my mother was going to kill me for being out so late.

I hurried home as quickly as I could, but I admit that I kept glancing over my shoulder the whole time. The still night air seemed *wrong* somehow, different than before, though I couldn't put my finger on why. I couldn't shake the feeling that somebody was watching either, but the roads behind me had been dark and empty.

Finally, the moment I had been truly dreading arrived - I saw the lights of my house and nervously opened our creaking wooden gate.

Mother, as expected, had been furious, not to mention nearly beside herself with worry. I tried to sneak into the house through the back door, but she had been waiting and pounced on me like a cat as I entered. With her eyes blazing and a long accusing finger pointing directly at me, she quickly forbade me from going out for a whole week, and had even strung small pouches of St John's wort, rowan berries and iron nails around my window and door in case any of the Fae came searching for me.

I had expected her to forget the whole incident in time, but she had gone on to hang those pouches all around the house, and to refresh the contents each and every year whilst I had lived and grown up there. They were still there when I eventually left home, moving away to the city and the job that waited for me there. It was a surprise then – though in hindsight I suppose it shouldn't have been – when I finally came home again nine years later, shortly after her sudden passing, to find they were still firmly in place and had apparently been freshly changed earlier that same year.

I returned alone to the house where I had grown up, a mixture of strong emotions battling within me: guilt and regret that I had not been back to visit, amazement at how much smaller the house now seemed, and a curious sense of warped familiarity at how so little had changed whilst also feeling so very different. I had stayed in touch with mother over the phone of course, and had always been diligent to call, but my job had swept me away and life too had derailed the best of intentions. Like a fast-flowing river it had carried me swiftly off into a new world full of deadlines, friends, trips abroad and romance, and the years had raced past with a speed I had barely thought possible. But, as I eventually discovered, there were rocks and treacherous undercurrents in that river too - the romance had ended upon them, and my job had been dragged suddenly beneath the waters, drowned by a crippling recession.

That had been the time when I had decided to come home, seeking the wide green fields and quiet country pathways I had so loved as a child, wanting to escape from the cold steel and concrete of the choking and frenetic city. And ironically, it was as I had reached this decision that the call about my mother's death had come, adding to my misery and sense of utter dislocation with a world that now seemed more fragile and uncertain than ever before.

The first thing I did after dropping off my bags at the house and quickly checking the old place over, was to head for the small churchyard at the heart of the village. It was strange walking those country lanes again. After stepping through the old lych-gate, I quickly found her grave resting alone in a secluded part of the cemetery, close to an old yew who cast its dark shadow across her grave. She didn't yet have a headstone installed, and only a small temporary plaque bore her name.

I stood in silence, lost deeply in bittersweet thoughts and memories as the reality of her death finally hit me like a physical blow. I don't know how long I stood there, the concept of time suddenly ceased to have any meaning. It was a strange feeling given that so much of my recent life had been a slave to the clock: tightly organised and bound by deadlines and timetables and appointments. In the village time assumed less of an importance. Here the cycle of the seasons dictated the organisation of the world, guided the planting and the harvest, the lambing and the tasks of the year.

Standing in that tranquil graveyard, the bright June sun filtering through the trees and forming dappled pools of light across the neatly trimmed grass, I felt oddly like I had been reborn. Breathing in the sweet and fragrant morning air that seemed so pure and fresh after having spent so long in the traffic-fume air of the city was like an elixir that filled me with renewed vitality, and even in my pain and sorrow I felt more alive and connected to the world than I had in years.

"Graham?" A voice I half remembered called out, and I turned to see an elderly man and woman standing nearby. It took me a moment to recognize them as Herbert and Ethel – the couple who lived across from the churchyard and who had always given me sweets at Easter when I had been growing up.

"It *is* you!" Herbert smiled warmly, "I didn't know you were home. When did you get back?"

"You're looking well," Ethel added with a motherly smile before I even had a chance to answer.

"Just a short time ago, and thanks."

"We were so sorry to hear of your mother's passing," Herbert said, casting a respectful glance at the grave.

"But we all knew it was her time," his wife explained gently, reaching out to pat my arm in a comforting manner. "We heard the wail of the *Bean Sidhe* in the night, over your house, and we just knew."

Herbert looked suddenly embarrassed and gave a quick admonishing glance at his wife, as though worried I might be hurt or offended by her words. Instead, I had a curious sense of remembrance. It had been so long since I had heard anyone speak of the Sidhe, I had almost forgotten all about them. My life in the city had made me forget so much of the lore and tales I had heard as a boy, and had taught me look at such things as mere superstition. This was not the age of faeries and magic, I mused bitterly, it was the age of human dominance over nature, the brutal taming of the world to suit our selfish needs. The Earth, once cherished and held sacred by many cultures, was now ours to exploit, and the religion of our age was the car and the computer, and money alone opened the mysteries and filled our lives with meaning. Anything else had just been dismissed as old wives' tales or childish folklore.

But suddenly there they were again, the Sidhe, and with that thought came the immediate recollection of the night I had fallen asleep under the old oak, snapping back into my mind like somebody hitting a light switch, and bringing with it the clarity and vividness as if it had just happened. How could I have forgotten?

"Well, we'd best be on our way. Good to have you back," Herbert had said quickly, looking extremely uncomfortable as he hurried his wife away. He muttered unhappily to her as they crossed the road, and I guess he had taken the stunned look on my face for shock or grief about my mother, when in reality my thoughts were still filled with memories of that night so long ago.

My next stop, unsurprisingly, was Sidhe Brook. Very little had changed in the time I had been away. The place was still wild and untamed, and the signs of modern life had not encroached upon it at all. The road was still little more than a track and the hedgerows and grassy hills still blossomed with a verdant array of wildflowers and plants. At this time of year the haze of summer was upon everything, and the dense, coiling brambles were thick with ripening blackberries. The warm noon air was filled with bees and small flies that buzzed in profusion around the berries and plants whose sweet scents filled every breath I took and which acted like a drug upon my senses, making my eyes drowsy and heavy.

I sat on the dry grass near to the old bridge, enjoying the sunlight on my face and feeling it warm my body as I relaxed. Two magpies fluttered down into the road close by, glancing at me in surprised alarm as I shifted slightly, and then they were off – wheeling overhead into the clear blue sky; and it was then, as I watched them go, that I became aware of a presence behind me.

In that moment I suddenly recalled all the old stories about that ancient hawthorn which sat a little way behind me near the rough ring of toadstools.

I froze at the sound of something moving softly through the whispering grass, and a cold chill ran through my body despite the heat of the day.

It's probably just a fox or a bird, I told myself, trying to pluck up the courage to turn and look, *maybe even a rabbit or a hare.*

But I knew in my heart it wasn't. Surely no fox would ordinarily approach this close to a human, and I knew the timid hares and rabbits would have also turned and fled at the sight of me – but whatever I was hearing was moving *toward* me with a steady and deliberate tread.

I swallowed hard, an uneasy crawling growing in the pit of my stomach. Suddenly it was as though I were a child again, clothes covered in burs, crouching under the old oak in the dead of night and shivering in wonder and fear.

The sounds of movement stopped and the whispering grass was still. I sensed something behind me, waiting and watching, and the crawling sensation in my stomach grew more intense. My heart was pounding and my palms were slick with sweat. I swallowed dryly and turned slowly, the act seeming to take more of a deliberate effort than usual, and looked behind me.

There was nobody there.

Feeling both relieved and more than a little foolish, I breathed out a sigh of relief – but then my eye spotted something dark lying in the grass behind me. It was a bracelet made of elderberries that had been carefully strung onto a silvery gossamer thread. I picked it up and glanced around, wondering if it had been there when I had first sat down. Carefully slipping the fragile bracelet into my pocket, I climbed to my feet and made my way quickly home.

I had a restless night that evening, tossing and turning as I struggled to get to sleep. But my mind was racing with thoughts and ideas, and I couldn't seem to shut it down. Finally, admitting defeat, I had kicked the sweat-soaked covers aside in the early hours of the morning and made my way down to the kitchen where I fixed myself a cup of camomile tea before sitting at the table with my head in my hands.

Blearily I peered over at the clock though eyes ready to pop out of my head, and sighed. The tea wasn't helping, and the thoughts still buzzed like a restless swarm of bees in my mind. Foremost amongst them were the questions of what I would do now? Where would I find work? And should I stay in the village or move on?

With a frustrated groan I rose from the table and carried the cold dregs of my tea over to the sink, peering quickly up at my own weary reflection in the glass of the window.

As I did, it felt like a cold hand had suddenly seized my heart.

A different face was staring back in at me from outside.

For a second I blinked, sure it was just my own reflection distorted by the glass. Then the icy shiver returned as I knew it was not. The cup dropped from my hands, shattering in the sink, and I took an unsteady step back, a trembling hand rising to my mouth.

The face at the window watched me calmly, unmoving except for the eyes which followed me as I backed away.

My world was spinning. My brain struggled for a rational explanation, and failed. My heart was pounding and my whole body was trembling.

The face at the window smiled faintly at me now. It was the same size as a normal human face and definitely female, but it was *beyond* human, with soft lips and shining eyes, and a wild and untamed quality to it. It was the face of a being that has walked in worlds and realms other than our own, and known secrets older than humanity. A slender hand now appeared next to it and rapped lightly on the glass of the window three times, and then the figure beckoned softly to me.

I opened my mouth to speak, but nothing came, only a strangled-sounding wheeze. My whole body seized up on me, and my mind was spinning in a circle, trying to process what it was seeing against the rational and everyday experiences of my life so far.

And then she was gone, so fast it took a moment for me to realise it. I stared at the empty patch of window like a man in a daze. I was afraid to blink, afraid to move, and unsure of what to do next. Had I really seen it, or had it been some crazed delusion born of a mind starved of sleep and rest?

But then came the faint, haunting sounds of music drifting through the night – music I had not heard in years, but which I recognised instantly. The music of the Fae coming from the direction of Sidhe Brook, and suddenly I understood what I had seen, and just what it meant.

The morning found me sitting alone at the kitchen table, staring sightlessly down at the old varnished wooden surface, a new set of questions flooding through my mind. That face at the window haunted my thoughts – so proud and beautiful, and so filled with power and life. A far cry from the twee and hideously fluffy 'fairies' found in Disney cartoons and popular culture, with their tiny bodies, childlike faces and glittering wings. I had never seen a Sidhe before, but still, I knew that's what it had been.

How much had we forgotten during the relentless march of our 'advancement' as a species? How blind had we become in the arrogant and blinkered delusion that we understood all there was to know about the world, or that science alone could reveal the answers to everything?

My mother had always been known as something of a 'cunning woman' in the village, making herbal cures to help sick children and crafting charms of berries and herbs to ward off ill luck and unwelcome spirits. We even had an old witch bottle bricked up into the wall by the hearth which she had once told me had been made by her own mother.

But she had never forced her beliefs onto me, and admittedly I had never shown much interest in learning about herbs and stones, trees and charms. I had still picked up scattered fragments of her knowledge however, for she had taken great pains to warn me which flowers and plants were safe, and which mushrooms were edible and which were not. I knew to avoid the rue in our garden when the sunlight had been upon it, and to ignore the dangerous seduction of the dark berries of belladonna when out picking blackberries and other fruits. But I now understood how much had been lost with her passing, and I was starting to fear that I might be in a situation I was ill-equipped to deal with without her guidance and knowledge. I was thankful that I had left her protective charms in place –

those nails and pouches of herbs that were strung over every door and window, and above the fireplaces.

I spent the day in the house, afraid to go out. I kept away from the windows, though I would occasionally risk a quick glance at them. I was like a rabbit trapped in its warren with the fox prowling outside, and despite some part of my mind struggling to convince me I must be missing a totally rational explanation, I had no doubts that the Sidhe would come back for me once the moon had risen. Mother had always insisted that I was marked by them – ever since that night when, as a child, they had spotted me trying to spy on their dance. I had never truly believed her, until now.

The ticking of the old clock above the hearth cast a spell upon me throughout that day, reminding me of the constant and unstoppable ebbing of time and heralding with each note the approach of the dusk and my own deepening unease. But even though I knew they couldn't come into the house – not with the charms in place, I was still alone, helpless and terrified to be the target of forces beyond my understanding.

I finally fell asleep from sheer exhaustion sometime in the afternoon, slumped over the kitchen table with an uneaten sandwich resting beside me. When I awoke night had fallen and the light of the moon was shining in through the window. On the night air again were the haunting strains of the Fae music, and in a burst of panic I rushed to the back door – to check it was still locked – when through the glass I spied a figure standing on the garden path, silhouetted against the moonlight.

My heart lurched and a nauseous fear uncurled inside my stomach.

The figure was watching me, though it made no attempt to draw any closer to the house. Soft laughter danced on the breeze, like music in itself, and then my name was called in a sweet female voice.

I reached down and tested the handle of the door, reassuring myself that it was still locked – but my hand remained on the handle as I stared out at that shadowy form. I swallowed dryly, and then, without truly knowing why, I found myself unlocking the door and opening it just enough so I could peer outside.

"Who are you? What do you want?" I called, trying to keep my voice even. "Leave me alone!"

"You were the one who wanted to see," a voice whispered back. "I've been waiting for you, for so very long. And now you've come back to us."

"I don't believe in the Fae!" I said as boldly as I could manage. "You can't be real. The world would know about you if…"

"Your world did know, once," came the reply, "and then it forgot again, and we slipped out of memory and into legend."

"What do you want with me?" I asked. I dreaded the answer and yet, oddly enough, something inside of me yearned for it too.

"My brothers and sisters warned me not to come. They have little love for the Human realm, and little time for your kind. We have seen the way humans defile the land, seen the way you treat and abuse even your own kind, and we still bear memories of how treacherous humans can be. But with you, I sense a difference."

Against my better judgement, I opened the door wider. Despite my fear, some wild and reckless impulse had taken hold and was urging me to step outside. It was the same impulse that, as a child, had made me go and wait at the brook in the hopes of glimpsing the Sidhe.

She moved closer and I now saw her face. It was the same face that had been watching me through the window the night before. She was so beautiful and unearthly that it stole away my breath, and I stared at her, almost forgetting to blink.

"Won't you come outside?" she asked softly. "The moon is full and bright."

Some part of me was screaming as I stepped over the threshold of the house and into the garden, but I ignored it, giving in instead to the reckless impulse that now grew within me, supplanting my caution and my fears. I knew I had reached a crossroads. I could return to my mundane world and close the door on this beautiful visitor, or I could embrace the wonder and the magic being offered to me, and the unknown risks that came with it.

"I'll go with you," I said softly.

She slipped her hand into mine, and I noticed she wore a bracelet of elderberries, just like the one I had found lying in the grass. As our fingers intertwined it was like a blindfold suddenly coming away from my mind and senses. I could see and feel her wildness and darkness, her pride and her fury, but it was all bound like a counterpoise to her compassion and fascination with me. She was like an untamed force of nature, wild and free.

We moved soundlessly through the night like shadows, guided by the light of the moon and by the music that grew louder and closer with each step. And then, as we turned the bend in the lane that brought Sidhe Brook into view, I couldn't help but gasp at the sight that met my eyes.

About twenty slender and willowy forms were dancing wildly under the light of the moon inside two blazing rings of ghostly flame and within the wide faerie ring of toadstools that lay beyond those. Around the edges of this otherworldly circle of fire a dozen or so wild hares had gathered, watching calmly but attentively with their dark mysterious eyes as they gazed once more upon a sight that had been long forgotten by human eyes.

She took my hand and led us boldly through the flickering fire to join them and my whole body tinged as we moved through it. The hairs on the nape of my neck prickled and rose, but there was no heat from those flames. Her eyes were bright as she guided me, and that same spectral fire blazed there.

She led me in a swift dance, and we spiralled inwards to the centre of the circle. The cool night air caressed my face as we whirled and turned, and her sweet laughter hung on the breeze. The music grew louder and more wild, filling my mind with glimpses of far-off worlds, of deep leafy groves in the heart of sprawling forests and dazzling waterfalls and verdant cities rising from the foot of tall mountains, and my soul thrilled to these visions, yearning to step through the doorway to where those worlds waited. I lost track of how long we danced, it felt like hours, and then we were spiralling back out toward the edge of the circle. My head was spinning and my senses were reeling. My only anchor to the world was those pale slender hands that held my own. I was swept up in a rapture that I had never before felt, unable to break my gaze from her powerful eyes, and she in turn was laughing gaily, her long silky hair flowing through the night behind her like a silvery streamer as we whirled around and around, the haunting music of the Fae filling the night air all around us.

I staggered dizzily as our dance came to an end, but she kept her gentle hold on me, steadying my movements even as her pale eyes gazed deep into my own and a smile lit her face. My head was still spinning, and an almost drunken euphoria filled my body and my mind. I wanted to sing and join in with that beautiful tune, to cry out with the heady joy and wonder that built up within me until it felt like my lungs and chest would burst from it. But my eyes were now also growing heavy with the call of sleep. I fought it, wanting to stay awake and not wanting this glorious night to end.

I sat down on the grass and she sat beside me, whilst behind us the rest of the Fae continued their whirling dance.

"This is the third time I have come to you," she whispered, her lips close to my ear. "I will not come again. The choice must be yours. The doors to our world will be open for you, and although I could force you to come as others of my kind have done to humans before, I will not do that."

"What must I do?" I asked, fighting to keep my eyes open.

"Be here tomorrow night when the moon is again high," she said, "and I shall be waiting to welcome you."

I wanted to hold her, to take her in my arms and tell her that I was ready now. But my eyes were too heavy to keep open any longer and the darkness of sleep fell over me despite all my efforts to remain awake.

I awoke shivering the next morning, my clothes damp with dew, to find myself lying under the old oak where I had once awoken so many years before. For a moment I wondered if the events of the previous evening had been nothing more than some wild and fabulous dream or a delusion created by lack of sleep, but pressed into my hand was another delicate bracelet of elderberries.

I returned home as though in a daze, recalling little of the walk through the winding country lanes. The house seemed even smaller now than ever before as I walked through the front door, and I felt almost like a stranger there. I packed quickly, throwing some spare clothes into a rucksack. I didn't pack much else, for there didn't seem to be any need.

My last act, as the afternoon turns towards dusk, is to record these thoughts and these events, so that people will know what has happened, though I don't expect these words to be believed. As I write, I cannot help but think of the old stories and songs about Thomas the Rhymer, the famous bard and prophet who journeyed into the otherworlds after meeting the Queen of Elfland under the Eildon Tree. As I prepare for my own journey, I cannot help but wonder if I will ever return.

Some believe the Fae are spirits of the dead, others that they are spirits of nature. Some believe they are the old gods, and others a race of beings driven into the hollow hills by the spreading domain of Humanity.

Still more speak of their darkness, malice, trickery and deep hostility to our kind; yet enough tales exist to suggest they aren't all this way.

I don't know which version is right, if any, but I can feel them watching me, and I know that whatever they are, their existence is beyond doubt.

I have taken down the protective herbs and the nails and have opened the door to the growing dusk. I can hear again the music of the Fae drifting on the breeze, and also my name being called. Tonight, under the light of the moon, I shall walk to Sidhe Brook, willingly and alone, carrying no iron to repel them and no charms against their ancient magic. And as for what will happen next, only time will tell. And while I know the Fae can be fierce and proud and dangerous, I am not afraid at their call.

Instead, I wonder where it will lead me.

About the Author

Simon Bleaken lives in Wiltshire, England, and has long been a fan of the horror, fantasy and sci-fi genres. His work has appeared in *Lovecraft's Disciples*; *Strange Sorcery*; *Tales of the Talisman*; *Beneath the Moons of Zandor*; *Demons of Zandor* and in *Night Land* in Japan.

He has also appeared in the anthologies: *Eldritch Horrors: Dark Tales (2008)*; *Space Horrors: Full-throttle Space Tales #4 (2010)*; *Eldritch Embraces (2016)*; *Kepler's Cowboys (2017)* and *Best Gay Romance 2015 (2015)*.

He was the winner of the first ever short story competition held by the Museum of Witchcraft and Magic in Boscastle, and is a member of The Friends of the Petrie Museum of Egyptian Archaeology, OBOD (The Order of Bards, Ovates and Druids), The Druid Network and the Pagan Federation.

His favourite authors include H. P. Lovecraft, Clark Ashton Smith, Stephen King, Robert E. Howard, Terry Pratchett and Dion Fortune. When not writing he divides his free time between reading, combating a severe case of Skyrim addiction and even the odd spot of ghost hunting. He is also a full-time slave to two cats.

You May Also Enjoy…

The Politics Of Illusion
By Jane McCaa

Howdunnit? The Delians are the good guys, everyone knows that, so when they are accused of the serious international crime of energy theft from Chios, their neighbour and former ally, it shocks the galaxy. It shocks the Delians quite a lot as well, as their own investigations only seem to confirm the accusations. As the crisis deepens and war with Chios becomes inevitable, the Delian government calls on Zoë Arete to seek the truth at any cost. She is already being for trained for high office, but will her more private studies be enough to make the difference and save Delos?

Peace On Earth
By Jane McCaa

Whodunnit? The state visit to neutral Eirene is a major diplomatic coup for Delos, but when Zoë Arete and Peter Minyas find a murdered man in the centre of the capital city it complicates matters. When their investigation unveils an invasion, it complicates things a whole lot more. While they are taken hostage the crisis threatens to spiral out across the galaxy and re-open old hostilities. The brave few start to build the resistance but questions also start to be asked about where guilt and innocence really lie. As the struggle for Eirenian freedom begins, the true cost of peace will have to be faced.

Rites Of Succession
By Jane McCaa

Whatdunnit? When the yacht carrying Zoë Arete, Peter Minyas, their baby son and cousin Leo disappears in a space accident, it is not just a devastating blow to Delos, but threatens the still fragile detente between Delos and Sikulos and therefore the stability of the whole galaxy. Platon Arete's refusal to declare his daughter dead finds him increasingly isolated and his sole ally seems to be the Sikulan Governor of Eirene, whose own position is now increasingly precarious. Relations with rich and powerful Thebes are also deteriorating fast, with suspicions growing that they may know more about the accident than they claim. Can Delian society survive this?

Printed in Great Britain
by Amazon